MURDER IN VANCOUVER

A Northwest Cozy Mystery - Book 13

BY

DIANNE HARMAN

Copyright © 2020 Dianne Harman

All rights reserved, including the right to reproduce this book, or portions thereof, in any form without written permission except for the use of brief quotations embodied in critical articles and reviews.

Published by: Dianne Harman
www.dianneharman.com

Interior, cover design and website by
Vivek Rajan

This is a work of fiction. Names, characters, places, and incidents either are the product of the author's imagination or are used fictitiously, and any resemblance to actual persons, living or dead, business establishments, events, or locales, is entirely coincidental.

ISBN: 9798627124070

CONTENTS

	Acknowledgments	
1	Prologue	1
2	Chapter One	6
3	Chapter Two	13
4	Chapter Three	19
5	Chapter Four	24
6	Chapter Five	31
7	Chapter Six	41
8	Chapter Seven	47
9	Chapter Eight	54
10	Chapter Nine	62
11	Chapter Ten	70
12	Chapter Eleven	79
13	Chapter Twelve	84
14	Chapter Thirteen	92
15	Chapter Fourteen	100
16	Chapter Fifteen	109
17	Chapter Sixteen	118
18	Chapter Seventeen	127
19	Chapter Eighteen	134

20	Chapter Nineteen	141
21	Chapter Twenty	150
22	Epilogue	155
23	Recipes	158
24	About Dianne	166
25	Coming Soon	168

ACKNOWLEDGMENTS

To you, my readers, thank you for making me a bestselling author!

To those of you who work so hard behind the scenes to get my books published, thank you!

To my family, for urging me to follow my passion and without whose support these books would still be in my head, not on paper, thank you!

And to Tom, who's always there for me, thank you!

Win FREE Paperbacks every week!

Go to www.dianneharman.com/freepaperback.html and get your FREE copies of Dianne's books and favorite recipes immediately by signing up for her newsletter.

Once you've signed up for her newsletter you're eligible to win three paperbacks. One lucky winner is picked every week. Hurry before the offer ends!

PROLOGUE

Milton Arrowsmith, at the age of 41, was only just learning how to stand up for himself. But lying in bed in his luxury penthouse as the sun came up, and sleepily stroking his fluffy black Barbet dog named Louis, he had no idea how dangerous standing up for himself was going to be.

"Good morning, boy," he said to Louis. "We have a big day ahead of us today."

Actually, it would turn out to be the biggest day of his life, but as he basked in the soothing sounds of soft jazz, he was blissfully unaware of what a big day it would be for him. He had all kinds of the latest technology, and he'd set his alarm clock to play his favorite jazz songs on it every morning when he woke up.

"I wonder how tonight will go," he said out loud to himself. A thrill of adrenaline zipped through his body as he thought about it. A new empowerment. No longer was he going to be the Milton who people could walk all over, the Milton who people discarded as easily as they would trash.

He knew he'd been a docile, calm, mild-mannered man who had always turned the other cheek far too many times to various different injustices. He'd been that way as a child, too, with raging, violent alcoholics for parents. He'd discovered when he was very young that it was best to appease angry people, dominant people, and get on their good side. And it was a habit he'd honed masterfully over the years.

The only thing he'd learned from his childhood that had served him well was an absolute aversion to poverty. The flashbacks of sitting on the thin lumpy mattress in his bedroom with hunger gnawing away at his belly had never left him. There was no money for food, but somehow there had always been money for alcohol.

Those memories had imprinted a frenzied work ethic in him to the point he could barely function if he wasn't working. But it had spurred him on to stratospheric heights of success.

His luxury menswear brand for smaller men (as he was) had made him a multimillionaire. It had bought him a 6,000 square foot penthouse atop the Bellevue Pacific Rim Hotel in Vancouver, British Columbia, with all its marble, glass, and architectural features. It had even been featured in a magazine.

Milton allowed himself five minutes in bed, watching the sky change color as the sun rose. The glass wall he looked out afforded him a view over the city of Vancouver as well as the Pacific Ocean. While he was looking at the sunrise, he made a few short entries in his diary, as he did every morning.

When he was finished, he sprang into action, Louis padding along behind him on the sleek marble floors. Milton entered the cavernous, gleaming kitchen, and switched on his extremely expensive coffee maker. Then he stood by the refrigerator, looking at his handwritten list of things he needed to do today for what must have been the thousandth time that week.

"I think we're all set, Louis," Milton said, taking some cooked steak and asparagus from the refrigerator and setting it down in Louis' bowl. Milton had spoiled Louis with a very expensive and somewhat gourmet diet, and now Louis was very fussy about food. Louis wouldn't know what dog food was if it was placed in a bowl in front of him.

Milton continued to talk to Louis, "This fundraiser is going to be spectacular. Just you watch, Louis, I expect we'll make hundreds of thousands of dollars for the arts."

He would be hosting an art auction at his home later that evening, with his elite social circle of friends and acquaintances in attendance, checkbooks at the ready. He was an excellent organizer and everything was in place, including the caterers, the florists who would come and deck out the penthouse with flowers, and the large delivery of champagne and caviar he'd receive within the next hour or two.

After making his macchiato, he sipped it, looking out over the city and ocean through full floor-to-ceiling kitchen window. He let out a little sigh of happiness. After all the trials and tribulations of his life, he felt he'd finally reached a peak.

There was just this one last thing to get done, and then he'd have the Happily Ever After no one could have dreamed would ever have happened to him.

The doorbell rang and he slipped his phone out of his pocket so he could check and see who it was. He had a camera integrated into the door frame, and it sent videos directly to his smartphone.

"Oh!" he said, his heart beating faster. It was the person who he'd been waiting to confront. His final piece of the puzzle to his happy ending. "Just a second, Louis, boy."

He rushed out of the kitchen and into the bedroom, quickly pushed his hair around trying to make it behave, then he put on his most luxurious robe, a jade green silk one, and padded to the door in his exquisite Japanese slippers.

He fixed his face into a smile and opened the door. "Finally come to your senses?" he asked.

The visitor quickly stepped inside. "Yes, I have." They handed him a box of very expensive chocolates.

"Wow," Milton said. "You shouldn't have."

"Chocolates for breakfast can never be wrong."

"I might just have to agree." Milton led the visitor through the penthouse to the great room. "And what do you say we break out the champagne, too, given it's the day of the auction? Champagne and chocolate to start this very special day. What could be better?"

"I won't say no," the visitor said. "Will that wipe the slate clean between us?"

"It's going to take a lot more than that and you know it," Milton said, a smile playing on his face even though he didn't want it to. What he wanted to do was throw the box of chocolates in their face, but he restrained himself.

"Hello, Louis," the visitor said with affection.

Louis, busy with his meal, ignored the visitor completely.

While Milton worked on getting a bottle of champagne open, the visitor opened the box of chocolates. "I bought this one because it has your favorite in it, a coffee cream liqueur chocolate. I think there are four in the box."

"You remembered?"

"Of course."

Milton poured the champagne. "Although you didn't remember my favorite maker of chocolate."

"Oh no, I did," the visitor said. "Selene. But I thought that would be a little over the top. I wanted to give you something new to try. A new brand, for a new start."

"We can toast to that," Milton said.

He poured the champagne and handed the visitor a glass. The visitor picked out a chocolate and handed it to Milton. "Here you go. A coffee cream liqueur flavor. I myself will go for the chili dark chocolate truffle."

"You can have all of those," Milton said. "I can't stand those things."

"That's fine with me."

"So… to new starts?" Milton said, holding his glass up.

"To new starts," the visitor said with a firm nod, clinking Milton's glass.

They each took a sip of champagne, then ate their chocolates.

In all honesty, Milton wasn't sure that he really liked the chocolate. He didn't think it even compared with the Selene brand. It was a little bitter for his taste, but there was no way he was going to say so. He smiled. "This is simply divine. How's yours?"

"It's okay. Now, I really must go." The visitor downed the rest of their champagne. "I'll see you tonight."

Milton nodded, feeling desperate. "And then…?"

"And then we'll meet tomorrow and talk about everything," the visitor said soothingly.

Milton walked the visitor the door, then spent the next few hours preparing for the auction. He stepped into his large walk-in closet and picked out the suit he wanted to wear that night. He chose one of his more daring ones, again in jade green, his absolutely favorite color, with a gray lining.

In a couple of hours, people began to arrive, coming and going in and out of the apartment. The florists, caterers, wait staff, and the staffs of donors bringing over their very expensive artwork, sometimes accompanied by security teams.

There was so much going on he wasn't aware that one of the paintings that had been delivered had also been stolen. Someone carried it in, and someone else, someone he didn't even know was there, carried it right back out.

There really hadn't been time for him to notice, because late in the morning, Milton became very sick. He had to rush to his bathroom to vomit, over and over again. His chest felt tight, like a giant invisible hand had gripped it, squeezing all the air out of him.

"I… can't… breathe… Louis," he managed to say, before collapsing onto the bathroom floor.

He was dead.

CHAPTER ONE

Al De Duco, a former Mafia hit-man now working as a private investigator, and his restaurant critic wife, Cassie, absolutely adored spending time with Al's partner, Jake, and his wife, DeeDee, a celebrated upscale caterer.

They gathered together one beautiful spring evening for Al's last dinner with them on Bainbridge Island, located across Puget Sound from Seattle, before he headed for Vancouver. It was just getting warm enough to dine outside, and they settled around the table on DeeDee and Jake's porch, which had a beautiful view overlooking Puget Sound.

"Wow, DeeDee," Al said with a grin. "You pulled out all the stops tonight."

He was right. She'd made one of her staples, which everyone enjoyed, Beef Wellington. She'd prepared the fillet steak, coated it with a finely chopped mixture of mushrooms, shallots, and herbs which had been sautéed in butter and then reduced to a paste.

She'd wrapped it in a crepe to keep the moisture in, then wrapped it in parma ham and puff pastry before she baked it. She also made a green peppercorn sauce to go on top of it. For side dishes she'd prepared potatoes sautéed with garlic, asparagus with hollandaise sauce, and a butter lettuce salad. The meal was topped off with a peanut butter pound cake with a honey and cream cheese glaze.

"Ima thinkin' this might be the last meal I'd order if'n I was gonna' get the electric chair, the way you've laid out so much," Al joked.

"Al!" Cassie said, giving him a weak slap on the arm. "Don't say something like that!"

There was so much that bonded them – friendship, a shared history, a love of great food, and, of course, Al and Jake working together in their private investigation business. While Cassie liked to stay as far away from trouble and drama as she could, DeeDee had a fantastic investigative mind, and often joined Al and Jake in solving cases.

She was just as capable as either of them, and would have taken a full-time role in their PI business if she didn't love being a caterer so much.

"Aw, Cassie, I'm only teasin' ya'," Al said.

"I do think Death Row Catering would be a pretty good name for the business," Jake chimed in with a laugh. "Order a dinner, and we'll catch the local murderer for you. It's all part of the package."

"Why do you two have to be so morbid?" Cassie asked.

"I agree," DeeDee said, although she was laughing.

DeeDee and Jake's dogs, Balto and Yukon, big huskies, came padding out of the open back door and laid down in a cozy heap on the patio, their bellies full from their own dinner.

"Yer' gonna have to box up another portion for me, DeeDee," Al said. "If it's anything like plane food, Ima not gonna' like the train food."

Al had made the decision to take the train to Vancouver at the last minute, because their Mercedes SUV was in the shop. Al had managed to back it into a wall, and Cassie needed their Volvo to get around, so he planned to rent a car when he got to Vancouver.

"Sure, I can make up a care package for you," DeeDee said.

"Great. I'll be stuffin' my face while I'm lookin' at all the scenery," he said. "Thinkin' we should take a train vacation sometime, what d'ya say?"

"I think it would be a good idea," Cassie said. "I always automatically think of flying or driving. Taking a train never occurs to me, but it would be a lot less stressful than having to deal with an airport. I know there are a lot of train vacations out there, both in the States and in Europe.

"I saw an ad in a travel magazine for a spectacular one in Europe. I think it was a five-day vacation with a grand tour through Switzerland in a luxury train with fine dining. You'd get to see the Alps, drink far too much wine, then cozy up under a warm blanket on the train. Looked good to me."

"That does sound pretty good," DeeDee said. "It's about time the four of us took another vacation together."

"Count me in," Al said. "'Long as there ain't no killers on board. I'ma sick of 'em spoilin' our vacations."

Everyone laughed at the way he said it.

"Oh yes, those darn pesky killers!" DeeDee said, laughing.

Cassie had saved links to train vacations on her phone including the one through the Swiss Alps, and the four of them spent some time looking at them. When they were finished, they promised each other they'd definitely make it happen as soon as they could.

Dessert was a dark chocolate mousse cake with a generous splash of Grand Marnier, which they ate with a very expensive vanilla ice cream. DeeDee knew Cassie was partial to a good quality ice cream, so she'd ignored the shocking price tag at the specialty food store.

She knew you got what you paid for, and the ice cream was a thousand times better than even the more upscale brands at the local grocery store where she usually shopped.

"I think I'm the only one who knows next to nothing about this case," DeeDee said. She'd been very busy with catering preparations for a huge bat mitzvah for the daughter of a celebrity and hadn't had time to keep up with Jake and Al's business. This dinner was the first time she'd socialized with the other three in about six weeks.

The celebrity client had been extremely demanding, and she and her business partner, Susie, had been drafted (and paid, thankfully) to produce several mock-up dinners for the family and their friends to try, before a final decision had been made by them. "Care to fill me in?"

"Yep," Al said. "The lady's name is Philippa Murdoch. Swanky name, right? Kinda' fittin' cuz' they're swanky people. She talks like the Queen of England got lost in Canada somewhere. Her husband's name is Jonty. But don't 'spect I'll be dealin' with him much. She said he's got some fancy tradin' business meanin' he's never home. They're into all this modern arty stuff."

He rolled his eyes. "Ya' know, spendin' thousands of dollars on a coupla' brush strokes. Or a picture of a dot or somethin'."

DeeDee couldn't help but laugh. She wasn't a big fan of modern art either.

"If ya' ask me," Al continued, "ain't nothin' but a big con. Draw a squiggle in ten seconds, say it represents the… I dunno… fragility of the human soul… or whatever, and then flip it for a mil." He chortled. "Maybe I should get into the 'modern art' business. We'd be multimillionaires, darlin'," he said as he turned towards Cassie.

Cassie pursed her lips, stifling a giggle. She was far more tactful than Al, but she seemed to agree with him. "I have to admit that I prefer more traditional art."

"Anyways, one of their best friends got hisself knocked off jes' before a fancy art auction he was hostin'. One of the paintins' fer the auction got stolen, so it's gotta' be a robbery. They got a whole lotta' art themselves. They jes' want me to check out their security systems, get new ones organized, poke my nose 'round a little." He shrugged. "Seems like a standard robbery to me."

Cassie reached over and touched his hand. "Just be safe, Al."

"I will," he said, giving her a kiss on the cheek. "Reckon I'll be home before the week's out. Don't you worry 'bout a single thing, babe."

*****

The next morning, Al took an early train out of Seattle and arrived in Vancouver around noon. He was glad he'd brought the Beef Wellington and slice of the peanut butter cake along, because, as he'd predicted, nothing on the train's menu looked exciting to him.

Philippa Murdoch had arranged for a car to take him from the station to their home, which was in a very upscale neighborhood located in the center of the city. When he arrived, he saw her waiting on the sidewalk for him.

He didn't know how he knew, but he was sure it was her. Could have been that all the years that he'd spent in the Mafia had honed his intuition. Sometimes it had been that intuition that had kept him alive.

She had two dogs with her – a tiny little fluffy white thing in her arms, that Al thought was a Bichon Frise, but couldn't be sure. He wasn't a huge expert on dogs. The dog at her feet was black and had a lot of hair that almost looked like dreadlocks.

Al couldn't help but smile at the sight of it. Philippa herself was a picture of understated elegance, with camel-colored slacks, a white button-down shirt, and a Hermes scarf. Al thought she was probably in her fifties and very well-groomed.

The driver pulled up in front of the home and got Al's suitcase out of the trunk. "Al?" Philippa said, as he stepped out of the car.

"Guilty as charged," Al said with a smile.

She smiled back. "A pleasure to meet you." She nodded at the dog in her arms. "This is Penelope." Then she motioned towards the dreadlocked dog at her feet. "And this is Louis."

She walked over to the driver and said, "Do you have time for another trip?" she asked politely. "To the Bellevue Pacific Rim Hotel?"

"Sure," the driver said.

"Wonderful," Philippa said. "Al, why don't you bring your suitcase inside. I'm sorry to spring this trip on you, but Louis belonged to Milton, the man who was murdered, and he simply won't eat anything at all.

"I want to look in Milton's apartment and see if I can find something of Milton's for him to have for comfort, like a piece of clothing. And I also want to see if I can find any clues as to what he usually eats. You don't mind, do you?"

"Not at all," Al said. "Fine by me."

Before long, Al, Philippa, Penelope, and Louis were all in the car together, heading to the Bellevue Pacific Rim Hotel. Philippa looked preoccupied during the ride and sighed.

"It's so sad, my dear Al. It was only five days ago. Life was ticking along quite beautifully, and then... tragedy struck. Imagine, just five days ago we were all excited about this fundraiser, and now... we're planning for the funeral and wake this weekend. We're holding the wake at our home."

"I see," Al said. "I'm guessin' that means he didn't have any family? No partner?"

"No," Philippa said, and sighed again. "It's such a shame. He was such a lovely man, but never found anyone to share his life with. And he had his whole life ahead of him. He was just forty-one, barely more than a child. He had such an impish, happy manner about him. I can't..." She wiped away a tear that had leaked onto her cheek. "Do excuse me, I just can't believe he's gone."

CHAPTER TWO

While the exclusive Vancouver friendship circle didn't have a name, if it were to have one, it should have been something like The-Modern-Art-and-Expensive-Dinners-and-Haughtiness-Club.

And Paul Spears had never quite fit in, sort of hovering on the outskirts of the Group, but he was used to that, being something of an outsider.

He'd certainly never been prom king in high school or captain of the football team. The only reason he kept going to these events was Philippa. Beautiful, wonderful Philippa, with her gentle, kind soul, and dancing intellect and spirit. He would have followed her to the ends of the earth, if he could. He would have fought dragons and demons and run through the fires of hell, just to please her.

Yet she was stuck with that awful Jonty, who made cutting comments and rolled his eyes at her. There were plenty of rumors swirling around about his affairs, people spotting him at bars with this woman, or that woman, but never anything concrete.

Paul saw the worry in Philippa's face, though, and noticed how each time he saw her it was as if her spirit was slowly breaking up and leaving her body. She was becoming a shell, by an inch here, and an inch there.

Paul desperately wanted to rescue her, but the only person who knew that, other than himself, was dead. Milton and Paul had once been firm friends. They'd gotten close very quickly, then it had all fallen apart just as quickly.

And all because Paul had told too many secrets.

He sat, painting, in his apartment located a short distance from the center of the city, and worried about that argument. Did anyone know about it? Milton must have, with the huge mouth he had, blabbed on him. Were people going to suspect Paul killed him because of it?

His stomach tied itself in sickening knots, expecting the police to come banging on his door any day now. Or, even worse, they might arrest him at work. He was the Chief Actuarial Officer at a large insurance company, and that was just one of the things that Milton had ribbed him about.

What Paul had learned was that while Milton gave off an air of being docile and meek, he was nothing of the sort. Paul thought he was passive-aggressive, two-faced, and just downright nasty at times. And all with a wide-eyed innocence.

Although the Group had been meeting for nearly five years now, Milton was a newcomer to it. He'd only been in the Group for a year before he was murdered, and he'd arrived on the scene with an eccentric flourish.

Paul remembered the first time Milton had invited him out for a private dinner cruise, just the two of them. At that point, nobody was sure of Milton's sexuality, and Paul, being both straight and in love with Philippa, hoped it wasn't a date.

"Were you hoping this was a date?" Milton had asked him as soon as they'd set out on the water in his luxury yacht called 'Victory of Vancouver.' His eyes shined with mischief as he looked Paul's outfit up and down.

"You're not really my type," Paul laughed.

"Are you anyone's type? I've never seen you bring a plus one to any function," Milton said sarcastically. Paul, shocked by Milton's rudeness, tried to think of something to say, but came up blank.

"Oh, don't worry, I was joking," Milton said. "I'm just doing you a favor by telling you what other people might be thinking. I don't think you're a sad lonely person, it's just that other people might. I suppose it doesn't help your love life having such a boring job."

"I'm very proud of my career," Paul said.

"Oh, right," Milton said with a small smile, like he was humoring a five-year-old. "I'm sure you are. Now you're probably wondering why I've brought you out here for a fabulous salmon dinner."

"I'll admit I was a little surprised at the invitation," Paul said. "But I had nothing better to do."

"Of course you didn't," Milton said. "That's why I invited you. I sensed you needed some company. You're obviously a lovely man. You just need to come out of your shell."

His eyes lit up. "Look, I brought you a gift. It's something I like to call a confidence piece." He went over to where he'd put his designer leather briefcase, and pulled out a little package, wrapped in expensive paper. "Here you go."

"Thank you," Paul said, feeling somewhat amused when he opened the package and found a hot pink necktie. Hell would freeze over before he'd wear something like that. But he was a polite man and said, "Thank you very much."

"Naturally, it's from my collection," Milton said. "Not my personal collection, but my brand collection. I have statement pieces that when you wear them, people take notice and they fill you with confidence. This is one of them.

"You must put it on right away and replace that drab old gray tie you're wearing." He saw Paul hesitate. "No, really, you'll feel so much better when you do."

"I think I'll save it for later," Paul said, neatly putting the tie back in its package and sliding it into his pocket. "I wouldn't want to get it dirty with dinner."

The evening continued to be just as bizarre. But something happened that Paul didn't expect. He began to like Milton. Milton was a very good reader of people, and he let Paul know he'd seen the look in his eyes when Philippa was around.

"I can tell you're in love with her," Milton said, "and I support you. That horrible Jonty doesn't appreciate her at all."

"He certainly doesn't!" Paul agreed.

"I think she would leave him for you," Milton said, "as long as you make a couple of changes. I don't mean to be rude, but you're a little bit of a, how should I say this, beta. Don't get me wrong, from one beta man to another, there's nothing necessarily wrong with that. But I go for very strong men and women, alphas, who like to dominate. I'm happy to go along with that.

"The problem is that Philippa is no dominating alpha. She's attracted to dominating alphas, and that's why she's with Jonty. She sees you as a good friend, and nothing more, and she'll continue to think of you like that until you stand up for yourself and take charge."

This really got to Paul, because he knew what Milton had said was true. The problem was, he was diplomatic, kind, and calm to a fault. Except for the 'dark incident' he'd never told anyone about. Not even his family talked about it. He'd tried to bring it up once or twice with them, because he was worried that he might be a psychopath.

After all, he was very calm, which was supposed to be a psychopathic trait. And psychopaths were often first recognized for killing animals during their childhood.

Paul was about five years old when the 'dark incident' happened. His mother, having divorced Paul's father when he was an infant, had just married a widower, a brash and bold real estate agent. To Paul's dismay, this man had brought along his own son to join the family, a boy of six called Dillon, who was an absolute monster.

He'd been spoiled and mollycoddled his entire life. He had tantrums like a toddler did until he got whatever he wanted, and he was happy with nothing less than ruling the roost. Dillon decided what they ate for dinner, Dillon decided what movie they went to see, and Dillon even got Paul's big bedroom. Paul had to move into the small guest bedroom. Dillon was even allowed to keep a pet rabbit, Snowflake, in the garden, although Paul's mother had never allowed him to have a pet.

Happy-go-lucky Paul had slowly transformed into a very angry little boy. He retreated into his room, building model ships, while his mother tried to placate Dillon to please her husband.

One day, when he came home from Boy Scouts, he found his latest model ship, the best one he'd ever made, broken into matchsticks. Filled with rage, he went out into the garden and strangled Dillon's rabbit until it died.

Little did he know his mother was watching from the kitchen window, but she didn't make a scene.

Dillon had just gone out with his father for an ice cream sundae to 'calm him down' after one of his epic tantrums. His mother told Paul to get in the car, headed to a pet shop, and begged to be let inside since it was just after closing time. She bought a white rabbit that looked as much like Snowflake as it was possible to look.

She was deathly silent the whole way there and back. She replaced the rabbit, then knelt down in front of Paul and said, "This never happened, do you understand?"

He'd replied yes and that was the end of it. They carried on with their lives, and it was never mentioned again. But the event haunted Paul. He was certain there was something wrong with him.

Thankfully, Paul never mentioned the Snowflake incident to Milton, but he did mention his other secret – that he painted. He showed Milton his paintings on his phone, and Milton said they were wonderful. He even got Paul to send them to his own phone, and said he'd show them to some of his friends who were art dealers.

"You won't tell anyone they're mine, will you?" Paul asked.

"I promise I won't say a word as to who the artist is that painted them," Milton replied.

Milton was true to his word, but in a way that made Paul see the true extent of his character flaws. The next time the Group was together, at Milton's home after an art event, Milton began showing Paul's paintings, as depicted on his cell phone, to everyone in attendance.

"Some idiot sent me these, begging me to speak to dealer friends about getting them sold," he'd said with a chuckle. "Can you believe it? This trash?"

Milton made a point of showing the paintings to Philippa. Philippa said, "I don't think they're too bad, I actually like this one in particular."

"Oh, you're too kind," Milton said to her. "You must have better taste than that." He looked over at Paul, his eyes shining with malice.

And the way Paul felt inside, he felt like maybe the psychopath was rising in him, all over again.

CHAPTER THREE

"What are we going to do?" Lady Cecilia Tomlinson said in her upper-class English accent. She was something of a status symbol for the Group, given her English aristocratic background. But what they didn't know was that she and her fiancé, Brazilian ballet choreographer Gabriel Barroso, who was working at the Vancouver Ballet, were drowning in debt.

To put it more accurately, it was her debt, but because she refused to work in a normal job, since she considered herself to be a poet, although she was unpublished, he was the one trying to deal with it. And ballet choreography didn't pay half as well as most people thought it did.

Cecilia strode across the bare boards of her bohemian apartment, which was decorated with beautiful art, antiques, and items from all around the world, tears streaming down her cheeks. "We're going to have to give up the apartment, aren't we? And when will we ever be able to afford a wedding?"

"Oh my love," Gabriel said in his thick Brazilian accent, "I hate to see you crying. Remember, we have the painting to sell."

"Yes, but what then? That will hardly make a dent in our financial predicament." She flopped onto one of the low Arabic-style couches.

"We will find a way, I promise," he said. He came over to where she sat and pushed her hair away from her face. He looked at her with his large, piercing dark eyes, his black wavy hair tumbling around his face to his shoulders. "You know that if I had to live in a shoebox to be with you, I would."

Her face softened as her heart filled with love. "I know, my love," she said, sighing heavily. "After we sell this painting, shall we just forget about this life and go live in the tiny little village you come from? Maybe I'll have six or seven babies and walk around barefoot.

"You could be a farmer, and teach ballet to the village children in your spare time. Who knows? Maybe some of the ones from your home village would become star ballerinas. I'd stay home and bake and write poetry and get pregnant with more and more of your babies. What do you think?"

He was quiet for a long time, and then he sighed deeply. "It's just a dream," he said. "When you go to my village, you will understand. I've tried to get my mother and father to leave, but they won't."

Cecilia sat upright. "Maybe that's because they're seeing something we're not seeing. Maybe we're chasing after all the wrong things, being here, mixing with these elite circles who throw money away. Look where it's brought me.

"When I was in England, I was quite happy to spend my weekends riding horses in the country, and living a quiet life, with all my money safely in the bank. It's only since I came to this wretched place that I've made myself a pauper. No, worse than a pauper. I'm half a million Canadian dollars in debt," she said, and shuddered.

Her insides were burning. "Please, Gabriel. Why don't we pack it in, change our names, and start living the simple life?"

"No," he said finally. "We'll find a way through this. We will. Are you sure you can't find work?"

"Who needs someone who graduated with an anthropology

degree?" she asked, on the brink of tears. "Much less someone who hasn't used it for over a decade, and didn't like it very much in the first place. I'm useless, except for poetry, and there are absolutely no jobs for poets anywhere in the world."

"You are not useless, my love," Gabriel said passionately. "You're kind and brilliant and intelligent and resourceful and beautiful and everything else a person should be."

A lump rose in Cecilia's throat. "That's very kind," she said, her voice breaking, "but totally inaccurate. I'm a complete failure. I'm useless with money, useless at earning any, wonderful at spending it, and wonderful at qualifying for loans and credit cards with companies that should say no to me.

"And the reason is that I delude myself into thinking I really need that expensive antique or need to go traveling to the Caribbean for inspiration to write a poetry book. Poetry I might add that no one likes, and is getting no attention whatsoever."

"Why are you saying these things?" he said. "Your words are like daggers in my heart."

"I need to start being realistic!" Cecilia shouted. "All my life, I've been living in some romantic fairy tale. It was magical when I was a child, but I had my parents supporting me financially then.

"I had my romantic ideas about the world, and never thought about money being part of the equation. It was always just there, whenever I needed or wanted anything. I never gave it a second thought. And that's what's got me into this mess now. I can't support myself. I cannot… support myself…" She broke down in tears. "How… how… What kind of woman am I? In my thirties and unable to be a normal human being."

"Hey!" Gabriel shouted. He walked around her and grabbed her by the shoulders. "You stop it, and you stop it right now! There are a lot of people in our situation. Not everyone has it together. A lot of people go through hard times. Stop saying those evil things about yourself."

Cecilia was shocked by his outburst. She crumpled onto the chaise lounge, and sobbed her heart out, feeling the lowest she'd ever felt. "And the painting... the painting..." she wept. "What kind of people have we become, Gabriel?"

"Never speak of it!" he yelled.

"Never speak of it," she repeated. "Like we never speak of the debt. Try not to think about it. Sweep it into dark corners with the rest of our own emotional filth and dirty karma. No, I won't do it anymore."

"So what will you do? Kill yourself?"

"Maybe I should!" Cecilia shouted at him. "I'm just a useless waste of space who is no good for anybody, especially myself. It's a good thing I don't have any children."

She started to cry again. "Forget my stupid idea about your home village. I'm not together enough to be anyone's mother."

Gabriel sighed, feeling like his heart was breaking. Seeing the woman he loved like this was one of the most painful things he'd ever gone through. And he'd been through a lot, being raised in poverty in a tiny Brazilian village in the country.

There had been no electricity, and they washed their clothes in the river. But he remembered being happy, surrounded by the warm love of his mother and the guidance of his gentle father.

But this?

Gabriel walked over to where Cecilia was sobbing on the chaise lounge, and picked her up, one arm hooked around her back, the other under her legs. He carried her into the bedroom and gently placed her on the low Japanese-style mattress. She continued to cry and cry. He lay down beside her, stroked her hair, and looked into her eyes.

"Listen to me, Cecilia, you're not thinking straight right now, because you're feeling so bad," he said gently. "All those things you said about yourself, believe me, they're simply not true. Not one bit. You are wonderful and beautiful, and we will make our way through this, whatever it takes. I don't care what happens. I just want to be with you."

She snuggled into his chest, sniffing.

"This money stuff?" he said. "It's not as important as people think it is. You know what real life is. Real life is when your poems transform you to another world. Real life, for me, is when ballet captures my heart, and I am in a different realm. That's real life, darling. Without that, we'd be dead.

"I know people who are nothing more than the walking dead, wandering around, with millions in their bank accounts, feeling on top of the world. But they're dead, my darling.

"You, however, you're alive. So, so, so incredibly alive. You are passion itself. Maybe this world is not for us. For you. For artists. Maybe it is not designed for us, with its rules and regulations and skyscrapers and bankers. Who cares? We won't play by their rules. No matter how hard they try, they cannot capture our spirit."

Cecilia's body was pressed up against his, and they breathed in unison. "How will we go on?" she whispered.

"With pride," he said. "Knowing who we are."

She burst into tears all over again. "Thank you... for loving me..."

CHAPTER FOUR

Philippa, Al, Penelope the Bichon Frise, and Louis, who Philippa had told Al was a Barbet, entered the lobby of the Bellevue Pacific Rim Hotel. It was nothing short of extraordinary. In his mob days, Al had dealings with various shady characters who lived in luxury locations, but he'd never seen anything like this.

White shining marble covered the entire floor and walls, and modern crystal chandeliers glinted overhead. The ceiling was so high that the silver chains holding them up were taller than two men. There were no plants, but numerous huge silver modern art installations, some made into unusual fountains with water spurting and flowing in all kinds of weird and wonderful directions.

The furniture was different as well, with sofas that jutted out at a strange angle, making one half of the sofa's seating double the size of the other side. They were mostly black with yellow detailing and yellow feet, but there were random colored ones scattered throughout in bright tones – a ruby red, a sunshine yellow, and an emerald green.

But the most amazing thing was that halfway through the room, the ceiling disappeared. Al looked up and felt dizzy. He could see all the way up to the top of the skyscraper, where there was a huge glass dome showing the blue sky above. There were curved balconies lining the internal edges of the skyscraper all the way up with some pedestrian catwalks criss-crossing the vast space between them. Al had never seen anything like it.

"Wow," Al said. "So your friend rented a place from the hotel and lived here, huh?"

"Yes, well… not exactly," Philippa said. "He bought the penthouse suite from the hotel for his own use."

"Musta' cost a bomb."

They got into the elevator, which was the size of a large bedroom, and Philippa pressed the button for the top floor. "A bomb?" she said. "Seven bombs, plus your great-grandmother's soul, the future earnings of your great grandchildren to the power of nine, and your right arm."

Al chuckled. He had a feeling he and Philippa were going to get along just fine. "I get yer' point… Ya' said he don't have any family?"

"Not that I know of," she said.

"Where's his money goin'? Ya' sure some scorned relative didn't jump outta' shadows to off him and scoop up the inheritance dough?"

Philippa sighed. "I don't know. Why is the world so wicked?"

"Hey! The world ain't done no wrong," he said. "It's the people in the world. And I say half of 'em are good and half of 'em are wicked."

"You might be right."

"And ya' can't guess where that half's gonna' be. It ain't jes' that the good half are singin' in church and the bad half's rottin' in jail. Nope. In jail ya' got the goodies and baddies and ya' got the same thing even among the hat-wearin' church ladies. Ain't nowhere ya' can go and find only good people. Nowhere ya' can go and find only bad. That's what I always say."

"You sound like a man of a great deal of life experience, Mr. De Duco," Philippa said evenly, remembering that the person who had recommended him had mentioned how he butchered the English language.

"Ya' don't know the half of it."

"Perhaps you'll tell me your story someday," she said.

"Someday," he said. He didn't like telling his story if he wasn't sure how people would take it. Sometimes it made people afraid of him, like he was only pretending to be a reformed mobster and was close to putting a bullet in them at any time.

They finally reached Milton's penthouse.

"I'm gonna' sound like a stuck record," Al said. "But wow, again."

"I know," Philippa said. "I wouldn't be surprised if this is the most expensive penthouse in the city."

The little Barbet, Louis, wagged his tail with excitement, and ran from room to room.

"He's lookin' for his master," Al said quietly.

Philippa put her hand to her chest, her face clearly showing her anguish. "He is, isn't he? Poor little guy."

Louis' enthusiasm was heartbreaking. He let out little excited yelps as he ran this way and that, obviously telling Milton, "I'm home! I'm home! I've missed you so much!" but they just echoed around the cavernous marble and glass space of the empty penthouse.

"All I can say is thank goodness they've taken the crime scene tape down," Philippa said. "It looked so… wrong. It still seems wrong, though. Like Milton's going to walk through the door at any moment."

"Were the two of ya' close?" Al asked.

Philippa paused for a moment and looked him up and down, as if she were deciding whether or not she could trust him.

"Don't worry, I ain't gonna' think ya' killed him," Al said.

Philippa looked both shocked and offended, and Al realized his flippant comment may have hit too close to home. "Sorry," he said quickly. "Jes' my way of handlin' somethin' like this."

He was going to add, "*When ya' been 'round as many dead bodies as I have…*" but quickly stopped himself. He was starting to feel like stories of his Mafia past would send her clutching her pearls for fear that he was planning on taking them.

She carried on as if he had never spoken. "Milton and I weren't what you would call close, but I always wished him well. He was considered a bit of a character by our little Group."

"Your l'il Group?"

"I suppose you could call it our social circle. I imagine you'll want to look into all of them when you get the time. We can talk about them later. For now, I'd like to get out of here as quickly as possible. I don't know about you, but to me it feels rather eerie in here."

"What'cha need me to do to help speed things up?"

"You don't have to do anything," she said quickly. "I guess take a look around and see if you can find anything."

"Wait a minute," Al said. "The hotel must have cameras everywhere, in the elevators and all that. Surely they coulda' jes' picked up the killer on a security cam somewhere?"

"Unfortunately, there were scores of people milling in and out that day," Philippa said. "I would imagine that the police have gone through them all and questioned them one by one, although I can't say that I have a lot of faith in them."

"Why d'ya' say that?"

"They seemed uninterested," she said. "There's something of a wave of gang crime activity in the city, and there have been police cuts with the new government in power. They're stretched to their limit."

"Was he shot?" Al asked.

"I don't think so," she said. "I don't know how he died. I wasn't here when they found him, but from what I was told, there was no blood."

"They done an autopsy on him yet?"

"I don't know," she said. "We've been keeping an eye on the news, but so far nothing has been released. As I said, he had no family, so it's not like we can find out anything from them."

"How d'ya know it's murder?"

"Because a painting was missing. Actually, it was the most expensive one in the place, valued at $250,000 or more. That can't be a coincidence, can it? Anyhow, I just know. You can call it a hunch, but it's just a feeling I have, a very strong feeling. I know it's very unscientific, but I have learned over the years to trust my intuition. Besides, the police taped off the place right away. That's got to say something, doesn't it?"

"Yep."

"Anyhow..." She shivered. "I'd better go and find a piece of clothing for Louis, and I need to see about his food. I know Louis ate steak a lot, but he won't take any from me. Perhaps if there's some in the freezer... I just thought of something you could do for me. You could round up the dogs. Who knows where they are in this enormous penthouse?"

Al went on the hunt for Penelope and Louis, and had a chance to explore Milton's home in the process. He walked through room after room after room. Guest bedrooms. Empty rooms. Rooms with only paintings in them, like an art gallery. Breath-taking marble bathrooms. Dressing rooms stuffed with expensive clothing.

There was a studio with a half-finished suit on a mannequin. That and the dressing rooms were the only spaces that were messy, with multiple pants, jackets, shirts, shoes, belts, and socks all jostling for space and refusing to be in any type of order.

He heard Philippa yell something, so he ran back through the maze of rooms, his heart beating far too fast. "What is it?" he said, meeting her in the hallway. He'd automatically reached for his gun, and then realized, it wasn't there. Being a PI, of course he had one, but he'd left it home, not wanting to bring it across the border. After so many years of living by the gun, reaching for it was an automatic reaction for him.

"I found Louis," Philippa said. Louis was cuddling in a Milton sweater-nest in her arms. "The poor thing was curled up on Milton's pillow. Any sign of Penelope?"

"Not yet. Might spend days lookin' for her in this place."

"No doubt she'll be in the kitchen looking for a treat," Philippa said, shaking her head with a fond smile. "That girl never stops eating."

Sure enough, Penelope was in the kitchen.

Al was shocked when they walked in the room. The place was a total mess, unlike anything he'd seen elsewhere in the apartment. There were dishes everywhere, food was lying around, and silverware was scattered everywhere. In all the mess, it was hard to spot Penelope.

"No, no, no!" Philippa said, alarmed, quickly putting Louis on the ground and rushing over to Penelope, who was up on the kitchen counter, chowing down on a box of chocolates. Philippa snatched the box away. "Oh no! How many have you eaten?"

"Oh, man," Al said. "I know chocolate ain't good fer dogs, right?"

"Poisonous," Philippa said, frantically looking in the box. "I don't know how many were in here. Oh, Penelope, girl, what have you done? We'll have to take her to a veterinarian immediately."

Philippa stuffed the box of chocolates into her purse and picked up Penelope, while Al grabbed Louis and wrapped the sweater around him. They hurried out of the penthouse, rushing to get Penelope to a veterinarian before she died.

CHAPTER FIVE

"Penelope's going to be fine, Mrs. Murdoch," the veterinarian, a kind, rotund young lady, said. "Again, thank you so much for taking this seriously. It was only because you came in right away that I could induce vomiting and give her the activated charcoal doses.

"If you'd been even an hour longer, the toxins would have already been absorbed into her bloodstream, and we'd have been looking at a much more serious situation. I wish more dog owners knew just how badly it can end up for a dog to eat even a tiny little bit of chocolate, especially a dog as small as Penelope.

"I've just got to run a quick biochem profile on her, and if that's all clear, then you're good to go home." She gently patted Penelope on the head. "You're a brave, brave little girl."

"Okay, brilliant," Philippa said. She turned to Al. "I'm pretty sure this one wants to… use the bathroom. I'm going to take him outside. You'll stay with my Penelope, won't you?"

"Sure," Al said.

The veterinarian busied herself with taking the blood from Penelope and processing it. She looked at Al briefly and smiled. "So, Mr. Murdoch, will you…"

"Oh, I ain't Mr. Murdoch," Al said. "Al De Duco's my name. I ain't Philippa's husband. I'm her…" He was about to say PI, but realized Philippa may not want people to know. "Husband's cousin," he said quickly. "I'm visiting from Chicago. I jes' got here today."

"Oh, how nice," the veterinarian said. "Did you bring the chocolates, then?"

"Nah," he said. He didn't want to try to explain the situation to her.

"Normally I'd ask for one. You can see I'm a fan," she said, nodding down at her large waist. "But I'm a little wary after hearing today's news!" She smiled at him.

"What news?" Al asked.

"Just a story I saw on the news. Some fashion guy, I don't know who, he got murdered recently. On the news they said they'd found out what killed him. He'd eaten a chocolate that had been poisoned. You know, like the kind you get in chocolate boxes. Can you imagine?"

"Uh-oh." Al's chest tightened with panic. He looked at the box on the counter, the one that Philippa had brought to show the veterinarian. He looked at Penelope. "Was it Milton Arrowsmith by chance?"

"Yes, it was."

"Does that test yer' doin' there show poisons?"

"Some," the veterinarian said, looking up at him, alarmed. "Why?"

"Oh, jes' wonderin', that's all," Al said, trying to keep a straight face.

*****

When they arrived back at the Murdoch's home late that afternoon, Al thought back to the events of the afternoon, an eventful afternoon! Thankfully there had been no poison traces in Penelope. Philippa cried with relief upon learning the good news.

They'd taken the box of chocolates to the police station before coming home. They had no way of knowing if those chocolates were the same ones that had poisoned Milton, but they wanted to be on the safe side.

It was only when they got back to Phillipa's that she realized in all the worry over Penelope and the chocolate, she'd forgotten to get the steaks for Louis.

She knocked on Al's door and when he opened it, she said, "Sorry to bother you, Al. I think I'll have Beth, she's our housekeeper, prepare dinner. I could do with a bit of rest and a stiff drink. Do you eat Asian food?"

"Oh, yeah!" Al said. "Chinese, sushi, Thai, Indonesian, Filipino… ya' name it, I love it."

Philippa looked surprised. "Wow, you're very adventurous!"

"Hey, don't let the accent fool ya', Philippa," he said. "I know I sound like I ain't never set foot in a swanky place, but my wife's a top restaurant critic, and our best friend has a gourmet catering company." He grinned. "Believe me, I'm spoiled when it comes to food."

"My, my," Philippa said. "What do you think is the most interesting thing you've ever eaten?"

"My wife Cassie did a review of a molecular gastronomy joint. Ya' know, where they do a whole heapa' science in the kitchen. We had 'bout twelve different things, but I gotta say, the weirdest had to be somethin' that looked like an orange. Use your knife, cut it open, and there was foie gras inside."

"Wow, that is fascinating," Philippa said. "Jonty always tries to drag me along to those sorts of things, but it's never quite... floated my boat, if you know what I mean."

Al grinned. "Know what ya' mean, and I have to tell ya', although I did like it, it was more of a show than a meal. I went right out and got me a burger and fries on the way home."

"Ha!" Philippa said. "I'm a fan of something that's slightly heartier myself. Okay, I'll ask Beth to make a ginger flank steak over noodles. Would that work for you?"

"My belly's rumblin' already, Philippa."

"Great." She suddenly looked worried, and glanced around. "Jonty's due home at any moment," she said in a lowered voice. "There's something I meant to ask you, Al, when we were out of the house. But with poor Penelope, it slipped my mind."

"What is it, Philippa?" Al asked, leaning against the doorframe. She sighed, her eyes darting everywhere, showing just how uncomfortable she was.

"Looking at our security and ensuring we're not targeted is only half the reason I called you here," she said. "I was wondering if..."

"Go ahead," Al said with an encouraging smile. "I ain't gonna' bite ya'."

"Well, do you have any experience... investigating... infidelity?" She couldn't look him in the eye.

"Sure, we handle lots of those cases fer our clients," he said professionally, trying to put her at ease.

"Please keep an eye on my husband," she said quietly, then turned and walked away, obviously too embarrassed to talk further about it.

Al stepped back into his room and continued unpacking his clothes. The room, and the whole house, was much more traditional than Milton's penthouse. It was full of dark wood and warm textures, and there were many beautiful framed drawings of various herbs and flowers on the walls.

He took a little time and mulled over the events of the day. He shook his head and chuckled to himself about the opulence of Philippa's home and Milton's penthouse. He made a quick note on his phone to check and find out who was going to inherit Milton's money, and then he wanted to investigate his heir or heirs.

Al had always been a pen and paper kind of guy, but Jake was a little more technically advanced. He'd finally managed to persuade Al to use a cell phone app to note down investigation thoughts and details. It was set up like a mind map, with a big bubble in the middle, and as many bubbles as you wanted stemming from that, and then more little bubbles, going further and further out.

The app automatically shared the little diagram with someone else, so Jake and Al could keep up to date with their investigations. It helped, because they could each see things the other one had overlooked.

Al knew he was going to be too tired after a big dinner and wine to be able to get started on it. *I'll get crackin' on it first thing tomorra'*, he told himself. He planned to have Milton's name as the main bubble, then going out from there he'd have Suspects, Crime Scene Details, and Background info. That was as far as he'd gotten.

When he was unpacked, Al went downstairs to the living room, which was very grand and wood-panelled. He found Philippa there, sipping on something in a glass, with both Penelope and Louis at her feet. "I'm ignoring you, Jonty," she said tersely to her husband. "I've had a tough day and…"

Al cleared his throat to let both Philippa and Jonty knew he'd entered the room and was within hearing distance of their private conversation.

"You must be Al De Duco," Jonty Murdoch said. He was sitting in the bay window seat overlooking the street, and was wearing what appeared to be a very expensive suit. Al thought he looked like a model with his tan skin, salt-and-pepper gray hair, blue eyes, and white, straight teeth.

Hey, did this guy walk right out of a catalog? he wondered.

Al chuckled. "You make me sound like a celebrity."

"Well, your name certainly sounds like one." Jonty said as he walked over to Al and gave him a firm, friendly handshake, flashing his white teeth.

"Well, I gotta say ya' look like one!" Al said with a chuckle. "I'll bet ya' have to beat off the ladies with a stick huh, Philippa?"

She gave him a tight, polite smile, and Al quickly realized his faux pas. She'd just told him about the suspected affairs, and he'd gone and put his foot in his mouth. And, of course, there was no way he could apologize in front of Jonty or he'd arouse suspicion.

Nice work, Al, he silently berated himself, sending a mental apology to Philippa and hoping it wouldn't turn her against him.

"What can I get you to drink?" Jonty asked. "We're having a sherry, as we often do before dinner, but you're welcome to anything." He walked past the multiple bookcases, the grand fireplace, and opened an equally grand cabinet filled to the brim with exotic, expensive liquor bottles. "Take your pick, Al."

Al walked over and looked at the array of liquor. "That's what I call quite a collection." He pointed at three unmarked bottles, with different colored liquids in them. One was dark blue, one green, and one cloudy. "What are these?"

"Philippa's concoctions," Jonty said, a little dismissively. "She likes to make tinctures and herbal medicines. These are cordials meant to pep you up. Though I can't say I…"

"They all have different flavor combinations," Philippa said, getting up from her chair to join them. She suddenly seemed animated and excited, and Al had the impression that it was a great hobby of hers. "This one is ginseng and rosemary. This one is maca and acai berry, and the last one is kola nut."

"Wow," Al said. "Yer' an herbalist, huh?"

"Of sorts," Philippa said with a pleased but slightly embarrassed smile.

"My *nonna* was like that," Al said. "Whenever I got sick as a kid, she was always brewin' up some herbal monstrosity I'd hate takin'. I just hope your creations taste better than hers."

"If you don't like the taste, there are other ways to take herbs. I make all sorts of creams and lotions and oils."

"Don't bore him with it," Jonty said.

"Not at all," Al said, seeing a little of the passion in Philippa's eyes fade, although her polite smile never wavered. "So how 'bout that dinner?" he said to break the tension. "I'm starvin'."

"Sure," Philippa said. "Let me see if Beth's ready for us." She walked over to check on poor Penelope, who seemed to be fine curled up next to Louis, then left the room.

"Time to pick that drink, Al," Jonty said.

"I'll join the two of ya' and have a sherry. Ain't my normal tipple, but a change'll probably do me good."

"Sherry it is," Jonty said, pouring it.

"I'm sorry 'bout yer' friend," Al said. "Were the two of ya' buds?"

Jonty tipped his head from side to side. "Sort of. He was a good man who gave his heart and soul to the arts. I'm pretty busy with my work, so I'm not as involved in social activities as he and some of our other friends are. But I do my best to attend and give what I can."

Al nodded and took the glass of sherry Jonty offered him. "Gotcha'. With a killer art thief on the loose, all yer' friends must be worried right now."

"Yes," Jonty said, looking pensive. "It's strange how these things happen. Everything seems quite normal, just going along quite smoothly, and then something like this suddenly happens out of the blue. No one would ever have suspected it."

"So it happened outta' nowhere?" Al asked. "No threats ya' know of? No suspicious people bein' seen 'round?"

"Nothing at all," Jonty said. "It was very unexpected."

"Got any new people in yer' social Group?"

"Not that I can think of," Jonty said, "but as I mentioned, I'm not as involved as the others are. Some people actually have to go to work." He laughed, perhaps a little resentfully, Al thought.

Philippa came in and called them into the dining room for dinner. They sat clustered up at one end of a huge mahogany dining table that could easily seat twelve people. They gave Al the honor of sitting at the head of the table. Swanky. That was how Al would describe them.

When they were seated, Beth came in and served them their Asian beef dish. "Thank ya', Beth, looks delicious," Al said.

The young woman smiled, clearly delighted at being complimented. From the way Philippa was coldly polite and detached with her, and the way Jonty completely ignored her, Al suspected she was very grateful for a touch of casual kindness.

They began to eat. "This is delicious," Al said. "I know I'm here to check up on yer' security." *And investigate your potential affairs, Jonty,* he thought, then he said, "I'll start tomorra'. I wanna' dig 'round and see who killed yer' friend Milton. 'Cause if we know who the killer is, we can eliminate the threat. Plus, I got a lotta' experience, and I wanna' help ya' as best I can.

"Philippa tol' me Milton don't have any family. And, hate to be crude, but ya' don't know who his money would be goin' to, do ya'?"

Jonty shook his head. "I don't know anything about his will or even if he had one. But I did hear him mention in passing once that his parents were trying to get in touch with him. He said they were narcissist drunks who gave him a terrible childhood and lifelong mental health issues. He said he would sooner eat his own eyeballs than say 'hello' to them.

"I remember it quite clearly, because the phrase he used was so distinctive. Eat his own eyeballs. Conjures up quite the image, doesn't it? It came up in the conversation because one of our Group, Alexis Berry-McGuire, I expect you'll meet her, said she had stopped having much contact with her parents, since they always seemed to have plenty of toxic darts of criticism to throw in her direction."

"I see," Al said.

"You'll meet everyone at the wake," Philippa said. "I have a lot of organizing to do to get ready for the wake."

"Including tightening up all the security and putting away the paintings," Jonty said, looking pointedly at Al. "I'm not having a repeat of what happened to Milton, thank you. One would think having so many people around, caterers, florists, and the like, would make it safer. But we know from Milton's fate that wasn't the case."

"Right," Al said. "I'm happy to help."

Philippa bit her lip nervously. She only pecked at her dinner, like a nervous hen. And as it turned out, she was right to be nervous, because the wake would turn out to be a complete and unmitigated disaster.

CHAPTER SIX

Retired brain surgeon Ron McGuire wasn't a brain surgeon at all. No, he was a con artist and a thief and had been all his adult life. His name wasn't even Ron McGuire, and he had definitely never been a brain surgeon. But he was so entirely skilled at his act that no one would have ever guessed. He had all the correct fake documents and they had been created so skilfully that even the bank didn't blink an eye when he'd opened an account with them. He had numerous credit cards and huge loans he'd never pay back.

But it wasn't just the documents that allowed people to be confident in him. It was his air, an air of natural authority. He was sixty-five years old, tall, dressed very well and looked extremely distinguished. He knew how to put the right clothes together to look like the most important person in the room, and knew the right tone of voice to use so people would listen to him. He was very dignified.

He'd been Ron McGuire for the longest out of any of his aliases and identities that he had previously used, except for when he was a child and he'd been himself. He'd cycled through scores of identities since the age of twenty-one.

He'd killed a girl by mistake. They were play-fighting in an abandoned apartment building, and she'd fallen out of the window to her death. He wasn't about to stick around for the police to pin charges on him, so he'd skipped town, county, and state, shaved his long hair into a crew cut, changed his name, and dressed in a suit and hat instead of the cuffed jeans, tee shirt, and cowboy hat ensemble he'd previously been known for.

It was rare that 'Ron' would sit around and reminisce about his past identities and exploits, though. He was a man, like all greedy men are, with his eyes firmly fixed on the future. What could he get? What would his next scheme be? How could he squeeze the most possible money out of this situation?

He didn't even exactly know what he needed the money for at this point in his life. It was nice to be rich, and he had a large amount safely deposited in a Swiss bank account. He'd scammed rich women and banks, and entered into fake business deals, but now there really was no longer a need for him to scam. In all honesty, he just enjoyed it. He liked playing the game.

As soon as his beautiful young trophy wife, Alexis, left their apartment to go to her office, he rolled over in bed, snatched up his cell and made a call to his only associate, a protégée he'd trained himself over the dark web by the name of Hunter Stephan.

"Phase one complete," Ron said.

"You bet," Hunter replied. "And in style."

"Now for phase two," Ron said, then chuckled. "I've got a little acting job for you."

Hunter hesitated for a moment, and then said, "I don't know, Ron. I prefer the behind-the-scenes operations stuff, not being in the limelight. I like paperwork kind of stuff."

"How about green papers, like money, and a lot of it? You'll be paid more than a Hollywood movie star for the role," Ron said. "Trust me, it'll be worth it."

Hunter paused. "How much?"

"I can't be sure exactly. But ten million plus for the whole lot, half for you and half for me. Might be one hundred million dollars, might be one hundred ten million dollars. I don't know the ins and outs yet, but I'll find out soon. I just have to do some digging."

Hunter laughed. "I hope you're not scamming me."

"You know you're the only person in the world who's safe," Ron said, laughing along with him.

"You know what? I trust you. So what's the job? Who am I going to be?" Hunter asked.

Ron grinned with glee at his own genius. "You're going to be Milton Arrowsmith's long lost son."

Hunter whistled out a breath. "Whoo-eee."

"Let's meet and go over the details," Ron said. "You still in Philly doing the lottery scam?"

"Yeah, but I have someone to hand it over to."

"Let's meet in neutral territory, say golfing in California. Fly on a fake ID, any you want. I need to prep you for this coming weekend. You'll be arriving in Vancouver for Milton's wake."

In the lobby of the Blue Ocean Golf Hotel, Ron and Hunter embraced, like father and son. Being a scam artist was a very lonely life, and true camaraderie in the profession was hard to find. Given the nature of the game, it was very difficult to find people one could trust.

But Hunter trusted Ron with his whole heart. Ron, being older, more experienced, and more cynical, was always suspicious, and hadn't even told Hunter his real name.

They sat down for a drink at the bar, to run through their 'prelim info,' as Ron liked to call it.

"I know everything about this guy," Ron said. "You must remember, the key to being a success in this business is information. You need to have knowledge that only an insider would have. That's how you can pull off your scams."

He took a sip of his scotch on the rocks and looked out over the beautiful rolling golf course and the Pacific Ocean beyond. "Now, you know I'm a retired brain surgeon at the moment. No one in my new circle of well-to-do friends is a surgeon, or even a doctor, but I have read up on tons of brain surgery information.

"Why? Imagine what would happen if one of them brought a new friend along to a dinner party who was also a surgeon. He's going to want to chat with me about it when he finds out I'm a surgeon.

"If I'm not prepared, I can change the subject repeatedly, or say I don't want to talk about work, but this is a form of resistance, and it arouses suspicion."

"Uh-huh," Hunter said, drinking it all in. He'd gotten the same scotch on the rocks, wanting to be just like his mentor.

"The key is ease, not resistance. This means being easy to get along with. Being willing to share about your 'life story'." He brought his fingers up to make inverted commas.

"Be free and easy. But not too free and easy, because everyone wonders why you're so perfect. You've gotta' throw a dash of something in there to spice it up. Maybe drink slightly too much and tell them you go to AA, or whatever else. Act cagey for a few days and have everyone wondering, then spill a secret.

"You've got to make the people around you think they know your secrets and they have the upper hand on you. Don't make them hate you by being too perfect. Don't make them hate you by being too imperfect. It's a fine line to walk. A difficult balance to strike." He was enjoying the sound of his own voice.

Hunter nodded, as always, in awe of his mentor.

"So, let's get your persona down. We need a huge backstory. Obviously, we need the documents, birth certificate, etcetera. It's going to be a hassle producing a mother, so why not say she died recently?

"I'll take care of getting the death certificate. You could say you never knew your father and your mother always said you never had one. Then on her deathbed she told you the identity of your father. You did nothing about it, conflicted about whether you wanted to meet him, then you saw on the news that he had died, and you decided to come to Vancouver."

"Yeah, I like that," Hunter said, with nothing constructive to add of his own. Ron didn't mind, though. He was very happy to be the mastermind.

"We can say you hated your father, but you're entitled to his money since your mother never got a penny of child support. You can be angry with him, furious. It will make you seem more realistic.

"If you try to be a friendly, meek son popping up out of nowhere, saying you want to pay your respects won't work. People will take one look at you, think you're a fake, and that you're just there for the money. The anger would be more realistic.

"At some point you can break down in tears over the fact you never knew him, how he abandoned you and your mother, blah, blah, blah. Just be an emotional mess. It's appropriate."

"Uh-huh. I'm gonna' have to do some good acting."

"Don't worry. I'll coach you in all the tricks of the trade."

"Okay, I'll do it." Hunter said. "I promise I won't let you down."

"I know you won't. Now remember, when you first arrive, you have to not know me. There can be no recognition, but to make it easier, what I'll do is befriend you when you first get there. I'll take you under my wing, so to speak.

"I haven't mentioned much about my own parents to the Group, so I'll make up some story about having an absent father, too, and we can 'bond' over it. That will give us the chance to go off on our own so I can coach you more."

Hunter smiled. "This is going to be awesome. You said it's at least a mil, right?" His eyes lit up with obvious greed.

"Much, much more." Looking at how eager the young man was for a million, Ron almost wished he'd just given him the million as payment and taken the rest for himself. But bringing a young man into the trade was the most important thing. He drank the rest of his scotch. "All right, let's go play a round of golf and talk about the details."

CHAPTER SEVEN

"Trust me," Alexis Berry-McGuire said to the chairman of the board, Wallace Sutherland, in their private meeting in her office. "I am going to make this happen. I'm going to clear the way, then you're going to make me CEO. It's very simple and very straightforward."

She had a distinctive Southern tilt to her accent, a blonde Texas big blow dry (even though she was from rural Louisiana), killer high heels, and a very tight, very expensive skirted suit.

Wallace Sutherland ran his hand over her thigh. "It's as straightforward as you want to make it, Sexy Lexi."

She slapped his hand away. "My body is not for sale anymore. I'm a married woman now. I'll use other methods to get what I want this time."

"You talk so bluntly," he said, leaning his large frame back in the designer sofa. "What's a little fun between colleagues?"

"I don't have time for fun right now," she said, getting up and looking for a file. "This is a serious mission and I need to be in the right frame of mind." She opened the file and was about to read from it.

"Look, don't tell me too much about it," he said. "I don't want to know all the gory details. Just get the job done, come back, and I'll persuade the board."

"Fine," she said. "Then let me get on with it." She looked at him and softened for a moment. She was fond of the man, in a way. He cheated on his wife, he was underhanded in business deals, and had used extremely dubious methods in the past to win legal cases when he'd previously been a practicing trial attorney.

But she knew that was the nature of the game. Survival of the fittest. What was the point in playing fair, when someone else might choose to screw you over? You'd be a loser with nothing but your morals to pay your bills. Wallace hadn't let that happen to him, and Alexis wouldn't let that happen to her.

She couldn't afford to, and neither could her family back in Louisiana. Her mom and dad had never been rich by any stretch, but now they both had serious health problems and neither one of them could work.

She paid their medical bills and their mortgage on the new home she'd bought for them, even though she barely spoke to them, since their criticisms of any and everything she did made her feel small. When she was around them, she could actually feel all of her energy and confidence leaving.

Alexis paid for two of her younger brothers to go to college, and one of them to go to graduate school, as long as they went along with her choice of school and major. Her youngest brother Josiah was a high school dropout, and she gave him a good talking to as often as she could. But she was also practical and had money stored aside for him, too.

"He might not need a college fund, Mama, but he's certainly going to need a rehab fund," she'd said.

She looked at Wallace, her head cocked to one side. "Look here. Lord knows I love you, but I don't want to be this fun girl anymore. I want to be taken seriously."

"Come on, Lexi! Don't tell me I don't respect you and think of you as the 'fun girl.' For Pete's sake, you're not a secretary, you're the CFO of the company."

"I know, I know," she said, running her fingers through her blonde mane and sighing. "But is the board considering me for CEO?"

He shrugged. "Well, no, but we're not looking for a new CEO. Jack's handling things pretty well."

She sneered. "That Jack Trevino thinks he's the best thing since sliced bread. But say you were looking for a CEO. Would the board consider me?"

"Well, no, but that's because CFOs rarely make the cut for CEO. It's a different skillset."

"I've got the skillset!" Alexis said with passion. "I'm not just a numbers cruncher. I've got the social skills, the right-brained thinking, the creativity. I can do this, Wallace."

"I've no doubt, Lexi," he said soothingly.

"Well, you're probably the only one. Half the board probably wonders who I slept with to get the CFO position."

Wallace adjusted his suspenders cockily. "It was me."

She whacked him across the head with the file. "But I deserved the position, right? Tell me I deserved the position and I'm not just some eye candy that got lucky. That's what everyone here thinks, right?"

"No," he said. "That's the voice in your head called impostor syndrome. Look, maybe you wouldn't have gotten the role if I hadn't advocated so hard for you in the boardroom."

"See?"

"But," he said, holding his hand up, motioning for her to stop talking. "But your numbers have proven you were the right one for the job. You've made sound decisions, and everything's looking very good and bright for the company."

"Once I get the two others out the way, I'll be set. I've got one down, two to go."

"I've told you before that I don't want to know the details," he said. "I want to sleep at night. Don't get me wrong, I don't judge you. I'd do the same in your position, and I have done the same. But don't go blabbing about it to anyone, not even me. Do what you have to do, keep your mouth firmly shut, and everything should go well. You're a smart girl. You know what you're doing."

"Yeah," she said. She took a deep breath. It seemed he had more confidence in her than she did. She'd never done anything so dastardly before. The stakes were so high. If she pulled it off, she'd snag the biggest role of her life, the position of CEO of Icon X.

Their firm was the only company of its type in existence. They had designed and created the world's first in a mix between fashion and security. Their range of clothing included a bulletproof suit that looked just like normal office wear and which also came with a wire and a camera no one would ever find. For their next project, they were working on integrating wires and cameras into regular t-shirts and button-down shirts.

In their shoe category, they had a device that could be detached from the shoe and fire plastic bullets that could kill and were undetectable through security checkpoints using metal detectors. Officially, they only sold to police departments, the FBI, the military, and other approved organizations.

However, Alexis was sure there were shady deals going on, and their products were ending up in the hands of Russian gangsters and other unsavory groups. Of course, she didn't care. She wouldn't give a darn if the board served live puppies for consumption at the annual stockholder's meeting. She just wanted to advance her career by any means necessary. Heading up Icon X would be an incredible career move that would set her up for life.

But if it all went wrong? She'd end up in jail for life, or worse, dead.

"Wallace, once I snag the CEO job, I want 5% of the company's equity."

He let out a long breath. "Lexi, that's a reach. What are you getting now? 0.5?"

"0.7," she said, a sneer turning up the corner of her lip. "It's not enough."

"You're still pulling in a lot," he said.

"Not enough for what I'm about to do."

"I told you not to tell me the details," he said.

"I won't. Now go. I have to make some calls, and you definitely don't want to know the details." She said 'details' in his tone and accent, and thought it would made him laugh.

But he didn't laugh and looked very serious. "Don't make the calls here, Lexi, and be sure you use a burner phone. Good grief, girl, I thought you knew what you were doing."

Lexi opened her desk drawer and pulled out an old flip phone. "I'm not a total idiot."

"Good," he said. "But don't make the calls here or anyplace where someone could hear you. And that guy... Jack," he whispered. "I know he's gunning for you. So consider what lengths he might go to in order to hold you back. Including listening in to your conversations."

"Uh-huh," Alexis said breezily. "I've got this, Wallace, but thanks." She knew he was experienced in all kind of shady dealing, so his advice was welcome. She didn't generally enjoy people telling her what to do, or even make suggestions.

"Also, it shouldn't come to this, but cops track phones back to cell towers, even burners, so calls from here could easily be traced. Even if you just have the phone on, they can track it, so keep it off at all times."

Alexis flashed him a grin. "I've watched the same crime shows you have."

He gave her a knowing look, to show he was much more experienced in this area than she was. "Go home," he said. "You look stressed."

"I'm fine," she said tersely. "You go home to your wife."

"Ah," he said, with a little chuckle. "Is Sexy Lexi annoyed with me now?"

"Yes," she said, but couldn't help from breaking into a smile. "I'm going to go and make those calls."

They had a quick hug, his hands straying a little afar as they always did when they said goodbye. Then she walked down to the parking lot, got in her Mercedes, and drove out to a park where a lot of people spent the afternoon.

Alexis figured the busier the place, if cops ever tracked the calls back, the harder time they'd have figuring out who the burner belonged to. She didn't want to park in the park's parking lot, because it had a security camera that recorded licence plate numbers. She parked her car on a street with a meter you had to put coins into. Then she walked to the park, click-clacking along in her high heels.

She was nervous, and furious at herself for being so. What was she, some goody two shoes? She berated herself the whole way to the park, trying to turn the butterflies in her stomach into steel. Chaos swirled in her head, but she couldn't control it. Her body was betraying her, but her mind was set accomplishing her mission. She continued to stride along the sidewalk, telling her belly to stop churning.

Alexis confidently walked through the park gates, and immediately saw how busy the place was. It was a beautiful day with a sapphire blue sky and a gentle breeze. As a consequence, the park was packed with office workers, families, teenagers, and dog walkers. The next step was to find a secluded area so she could talk in private, but it looked like it would be hard to find.

It took her thirty minutes of wandering around, smiling at people and pretending to be enjoying the sunshine, until she found a spot. A sign outside a little gated area told her she was entering the Peace Garden. She ambled around it, surreptitiously looking out for people. There was only a mother and her young son, and they soon walked away, leaving her totally alone.

As soon as they were gone, she whipped the burner phone out of her pocket and powered it on. She punched in the man's phone number. He hadn't even told her his real name, just told her to call him Tom. She didn't like using that name, or even thinking of him like that. She knew his name was fake and thought it made her look like a fool to go along with it. She called *not-Tom,* and he picked up the phone almost immediately.

"It's me," she said.

"I know who it is. Don't say your name."

"It looks like everything went well."

"Yep," Tom said. "Payment was also received successfully, so thank you for that."

"You're welcome. Now I have the next part of the job for you."

"Shoot. I'm listening."

CHAPTER EIGHT

In the days leading up to the funeral and wake, Al must have checked every aspect of the Murdochs' security system a thousand times.

"Imagine," Philippa kept saying, "the person who killed Milton went into the hotel, under all those cameras, got in the elevator, rode all the way up, went into the penthouse when all those other people were there preparing for the fundraiser, then killed him with a box of chocolates, of all things! And then they still managed to steal a painting.

"If that killer is lurking among us, they're going to find it very easy to take out Jonty and me at this wake. I've sent Beth home for her own safety, so she won't be here.

"All you have to do is get through a front gate and front doors, to get inside the house. And being a wake, there'll be so much food." She became more and more agitated as she spoke. "And then people will bring bottles of alcohol along. We won't be able to drink them, Al, will we? You know, in case they're poisoned? Oh, I don't see how we can avoid being murdered!

"Okay, that's it, I'm getting Jonty to transport all of the paintings in the house to a locked storage room at the art dealer's. They offer locked spaces for temporarily housing artwork. That's what I'll do. Yes, yes, I will. That way, we can't be murdered. We just can't. Or...

can we? Oh, why did I have to offer to hold this wake? I barely even knew the man!"

She continued to be frantic, and in fact, became even more so, the closer the wake got.

"Al, check to see that the security cameras are working."

"Al, check to see that the door lock is triple locking properly."

"Al, what about the little courtyard outside? Do you think someone could jump over the wall and break in the back door during the wake? That leads right to the kitchen, and all the food will be in there, and…"

Even Penelope and Louis stayed out of her way, except during the evening, when she collapsed into her favorite armchair, drank a sherry with Penelope snuggled into her lap and Louis at her feet, and fell asleep.

When Al had first arrived, Louis had carried Milton's clothing in his mouth wherever he went, but as time went on, sometimes he forgot it.

"He's adjusting," Philippa had said wearily one evening. "I only wish humans could do so as quickly."

Jonty was mostly absent in the days leading up to the wake, and Al barely saw him. When Al woke up, he'd already left for work, and he often came home at 10:00 at night, took his dinner plate into his home office, and wasn't seen again for the rest of the night.

Al wondered if he was just a workaholic, or if he was having an affair, as Philippa suspected. There was actually little to no time to investigate that issue, since Philippa's demands were constant. She asked him to do the same task over and over, and even when he pointed it out, she said, "Would you please just check it again, Al, dear?"

"Sure," he'd say with a smile, then go to wherever it was that she wanted something done. But he wouldn't do the work she'd asked. He was trying to track down Milton's family with the help of Jake and DeeDee, who he kept in touch via WhatsApp and email.

Check into Arrowsmiths, he'd written them. *Shouldn't be a big problem.*

Because they were licensed private investigators, they had special access to national records for both the U.S. and Canada. They were able to obtain census records, property records, driving records, criminal records, marriage records, and birth and death certificates.

They found Milton Arrowsmith's parents, a Jean James and Uriel Arrowsmith. But the trail on both of them went cold in the early 2000s. And there were no death records for either of them.

Looks like they've gone off the radar, Jake had written Al in an email. *Maybe they went to live in another country?*

Al told Jake to try to get access to the international records, but they both knew the chances of finding them in such a limited time was slim. If someone hadn't been married or died in the new country, then they'd be very difficult to track down with a preliminary search.

Besides, Al barely got any time to himself. No sooner was he out of sight for more than twenty minutes then he'd hear Philippa calling out, "Al! Al! Where are you?"

By the night before the wake, Al was thoroughly sick of the sight and sound of her. It was then that Philippa and Jonty had a very bad argument. Usually by the time he rolled in the door she was drooping in her armchair, ready to head to bed, but that night, she was still cleaning the already clean house, and she met him at the door, the feather duster in her hand looking like a weapon.

"Jonathan!" she yelled at him. "I've been telling you to get those paintings transported every single day, multiple times, for the past I don't know how long. And they're your precious collection."

He barged right past her without a word, and went into the kitchen.

"Ignoring me, are you?" Philippa said. Al was worried when he looked at her. Her eyes bulged with rage, her skin was reddening by the moment, and she looked capable of committing murder. Al had no doubt she was considering strangling Jonty with her bare hands.

Jonty poured himself a soda from the refrigerator, and gave Al an apologetic look, as if to say, *sorry my wife is such a freaking nutcase.*

Al said, "Philippa, don't worry. I'll take care of the paintins'."

Normally, Philippa would have been very polite and kind to him, but not in this moment. She was too furious to even look at him. She flapped her hand at him, and stared at Jonty, who was avoiding eye contact with her with steely determination.

"Fine!" she declared. "That's just fine. I'll tell you what I'm going to do, Jonathan Aloysius Murdoch, to your precious paintings. I'm going to go in there right now, with this knife…" She took a knife out of the knife block, "and slash them all into smithereens. How would you like that?"

That got Jonty's attention. He grabbed her hand that was holding the knife. "You wouldn't dare," he growled, his own eyes popping with rage.

Al could see this was going to get out of hand, and fast. "No," he said loudly. He rushed between them, grabbed the knife and put it back in the knife block. Then, being taller than either of them, he grabbed the block and put it up on a high shelf that neither of them could reach.

He used a firm voice and said, "Both of ya', stop this now. Do ya' hear me? Philippa, this house is extremely secure. Ya' know all the measures we've put in place. Jonty, yer' wife is scared and worried about what happened to yer' friend, and what might happen to the two of ya'."

Philippa burst into tears. "He's right. I'm sorry. I'm sorry, Jonty. I'm sorry, Al. I'm just... it's just... how can this happen? How can it? I feel like I'll never feel safe again."

Jonty sighed, then put his arms around her. "It will all be fine. It will," he said, though his voice sounded hollow, and it didn't sound like he believed himself.

"Hey, Jonty, howsabout you and me move the paintins' tomorrow? Or we could just put 'em all in one room and lock it up? Whaddya' think?"

Jonty looked down at Philippa who was crying in his arms. "I'll move them," he said. "I want Philippa to feel safe."

The paintings were moved the first thing the following morning. The art dealer's van was being used for another job, so Al rented a truck with a closed back, and they carefully wrapped each of the paintings. Jonty was in a jovial mood, and asked Al all kinds of questions about his life as he drove. Al was so comfortable he nearly mentioned the mob, but managed to hold his tongue at the last moment.

When they returned, Jonty quickly showered and changed into a black suit, ready to escort Philippa, who was in a black skirt suit trimmed with lace. She wore an elaborate wide-rimmed black hat. Sunglasses completed the look. Penelope was going along with them to the funeral home, and Philippa had even traded out her usual purple collar for a black one.

"I'm going to leave Louis with you," Philippa said to Al. "Make sure he gets his steak strips, and keep a very close eye on him. He might be able to sense this is his master's funeral. Poor little guy." She bent down in her high heels to pet him sympathetically under his chin.

"And, please, make sure you're invisible by the time the mourners arrive back here. I don't want them to know about my secret weapon and try to poach you from me. If you must come out, for whatever reason, please say you…"

She looked him up and down and sighed. "I don't know… how could you know Jonty and me in a social capacity? Honestly, it seems rather unlikely, doesn't it?"

Al got the distinct feeling she felt embarrassed by him and his accent, and the fact it was obvious he was not from an upper-class family like they were.

"I used to be Milton's driver?" Al suggested. He wanted to tell her where to go for her snobbery, but of course he couldn't. He had to finish the job.

"Yes, that'll do," she said.

"Don't worry, I'll be watchin' the live take on the cameras the whole time."

She clapped her hands. "Wonderful!" Then she yelled, "Jonty! Hurry up!" so loudly and suddenly that if Al hadn't previously been in the mob and used to bullets flying around, he would have flinched.

Jonty appeared a moment or two later, and they quickly left.

The caterers had already arrived, and were bustling around in the kitchen and dining room, but the rest of the house was clear.

Al, with a sour taste in his mouth from his interaction with Philippa, paced around with Louis, wondering what to do for the next few hours. In all honesty, he'd lost interest in finding out whether or not Jonty was cheating on Philippa.

And what if he were? With her crazy little episode of last night and her snobbery this morning, he didn't feel very motivated to help her out. He sank into a chair in the living room, feeling the hot burn of shame in his chest. Cassie was from an upper-class family, but she didn't go around looking down on people. Neither did her family.

Even though he was proud of his heritage and background, he sat there feeling like he wanted to disappear. He didn't fit in with these snobby types of people at all. He got the impression Philippa wanted to pat him on his head like he was one of the dogs. Her kindness hadn't been kindness at all. It had been pity. He just wanted to go home and the sooner the better.

He got out his phone and called Cassie. "Hey, babe," he said, trying to sound cheerful.

"Hey, love! I thought the killer might have caught up with you," she said, laughing. "You haven't been in touch much."

"Sorry," he said, regretting that fact. "The broad who hired me is demandin', to say the least."

Cassie paused. "You don't sound good at all, darling. Are you okay?"

"Yeah, sure," he said, trying to sound tough.

"Al?" she said quietly.

"Aww, I dunno. The woman's makin' it clear I'm jes' some kinda' second-class citizen 'round here."

Cassie let out a long, deep breath. "How? What has she said?"

"She don't want none of her swanky friends to see me." He cleared his throat. "Sorry, babe, I sound like a whiner. I'm jes' tired. Wait a sec, someone's at the door. I gotta' go."

"Okay," Cassie said. "Just… don't let her get to you, darling. You know who you are. You know you have a lot to be proud of. You're a kickass investigator. You're a strong man who turned his life around. You're an honorable, kind, and decent man. And very funny, too."

Al couldn't help but smile. "Sorry fer bein' a whinin' ol' man."

"Never!" Cassie said. "You were feeling down, and I helped you back up. If that's not what family's for, I don't know what it is for."

Al grinned. "True. Yer' pretty darn fabulous yerself', lady."

"I know!" Cassie said with a laugh. "Thanks, darling. Now, put all that investigating prowess into action, solve that case, and come back home where you belong."

"Yes, ma'am," Al said with a laugh. "Seriously, that's 'xactly what I wanna' do right now. Bye, Cassie. Love ya'."

"Adore you, Mr. De Duco."

Al hung up the phone with a smile, wondering what he had been so worried about. He went to the door with that same smile. But it quickly disappeared when he saw three very stern-looking police officers standing in front of him. He half wondered if his Mafia past had come back to catch up with him.

The tallest one had a face like thunder. "Is Philippa Murdoch here?" he asked aggressively.

CHAPTER NINE

Al stared at the police officers in the doorway with a look of disbelief on his face. Two of them were holding several large clear storage boxes. "No, she ain't. What's goin' on?"

One of the officers shoved a piece of paper in his face. "We have a search warrant authorizing us to seize certain items from this location."

"Please come in," Al said. He knew it was pointless to resist or ask them what items they were going to seize. But he was very interested, to say the least. "Got somethin' to do with Milton Arrowsmith's murder?" he couldn't help but ask.

"Can't say," one of the police officers barked.

They put the boxes down by the door and began to move through the house like a swarm of flies. Louis hid behind Al, but it was hard work, because Al followed them, desperate to see what they were going to seize.

They split up, and Al wasn't sure which one to follow, but soon, one of them called out from upstairs, "Items located!" and the other two hurried up the grand staircase, Al and Louis included.

They followed the voice into a tiny side room, which probably would have been an office had anyone else lived there. But it looked like Philippa's apothecary room, with herbs hanging up drying all over the place and bottles and jars stored around the room.

"We'll take it all," an officer said. "Load it up."

Two of the officers went downstairs to get the storage boxes they'd brought, and then they began boxing up every single item in the room.

"Does this got somethin' to do with the poisonin'?" Al asked as he watched the officers from where he was standing in the hallway.

The police officers looked at each other meaningfully, and then one came over and slammed the door in Al's face. *Man, I'm getting' disrespected left, right, and center today,* he thought. He walked away, but instead of getting mad, his brain started whirring into overdrive as he went back down the stairs and into the living room.

Did Philippa put poison in them chocolates to kill Milton Arrowsmith? he wondered. *Maybe she did. Maybe that's why she went back to Milton's apartment. To get the chocolates and dispose of 'em before the police could find 'em in the apartment. As it turned out, the autopsy had shown it was chocolate anyway.*

Al guessed they knew how to match up the compounds in chocolate with the compounds in the poison, since they'd have been released at the same time. Not that Al was a scientist. He left that to the experts.

But this was all starting to make horrible, horrible sense.

He slumped down into a chair and stared at one spot. That was what he always did when he needed to think things through. Louis jumped up on his lap and snuggled into him. He was too deep in thought to be surprised, but he mused aloud to Louis, "If she killed him, Louis, why'd' she bring me here to investigate?"

Did she really think he was that stupid? He was starting to get mad again. She thought he was that bad of an investigator that…

"Oh, but, of course!" he said aloud to himself.

It could also have been Jonty. But did he have enough knowledge of Philippa's herbs to accurately create a poison? He'd seemed pretty dismissive of the whole thing, but then again, maybe that was the strategy he'd used to distance himself from it.

But what motive would either of them have for killing Milton?

Al realized he didn't know enough about the situation. He'd been so busy doing a million and one unnecessary security tasks for Philippa that he hadn't had time to investigate. Maybe she'd done that deliberately, to stop him from poking around too much. Then she'd plant some evidence that led to someone else and have him find it. After thinking about it for some time, he became incensed.

The police left shortly afterward. Did they know it was her? Probably not. If they needed the warrant to seize the herbal collection, then they must need to have it analyzed. He wondered what they were looking for.

Al slid his smartphone out of his pocket and searched *Milton Arrowsmith poisoning chocolate*. A number of search results came up from news sites. He tapped on the first one, and scanned the article, looking for the name of the poison. He had to wade through a lot of details, but finally he found it.

Ricin.

He didn't need to hit Google again. He knew exactly what ricin was from his days in the mob. His boss once had a "Bulgarian umbrella" made for him. Al was in charge of its delivery from the backstreet maker to the boss, who had gotten the idea from a Cold War tactic used by the Bulgarian Secret Service.

It was an actual umbrella, with a poisonous pellet of ricin embedded in the tip, which was hollowed out like a gun chamber.

There was a little button on the umbrella handle that worked as a trigger, sending the poisoned pellet flying out at a high rate of speed.

It would lodge in the victim's body, and depending on how much ricin was included, the victim's death would happen in a space of three hours to five days.

But Al didn't know what ricin was made from. He researched how to make ricin, and hoped that didn't bring him up on some government search list and his smartphone would be monitored from then on.

He found out it was made from castor beans. An article he found about ricin-laced envelopes being sent to the President told him it was easy to do. The beans are soaked and cooked, mashed and filtered, then soaked in a solvent. Although it was dangerous, it could be done at home.

Philippa would have had more than enough time to do it, but what about Jonty?

Al's body, without consulting his mind, stood up and went to Jonty's office. Al figured if Jonty had made the poison, it would have been in his office. Maybe he'd left behind evidence of some kind. Al tried the door handle. It stubbornly shifted from side to side and wouldn't turn. The door was locked.

A voice called out from the hallway. A female with an English accent, and in a happy tone of voice said, "Hellooo? Is anybody there? Yoohoo!"

Al walked around the corner to find a very unusual looking woman standing at the open front door. She had on a loose jade green caftan, and her hair was wrapped up in a black velvet turban, which made her skin look very pale. She wore large rings on each finger, and kind of reminded Al of a fortune teller, or somebody dressing up as one. But she wore a cheerful smile, and Al got the immediate impression she was a "good person."

"Hey," Al said, not being able to stop himself from smiling in response to her own silly smile. "How are ya'?" He remembered Philippa's warning not to let anyone know who he was. "I'm Al, Milton's former driver."

She frowned. "No, you're not. Clyde was his last driver."

"Before Clyde."

"No, that was Alex."

"Yeah," Al said. "That's me. Alex. Al."

She frowned at him and crossed her arms. "Are you going to tell me who you really are?" She looked down at Louis and said, "You may as well say he was Milton's driver. Wait, isn't that Louis?"

He sighed and put his hands up. "Ya' got me. I'm security for the paintins' in the house. I'm from the art gallery. I jes' said I was the driver 'cause people ain't supposed to know who security is. Don't tell anyone."

He nodded down at Louis. "And as fer this l'il guy, Mrs. Murdoch's taken him in, and the poor soul's gotten attached to me." He shrugged. "No accountin' for taste. And who are you?"

"I'm Cilly. That's like the word silly, but with a c. Cecilia Tomlinson, really, but don't call me Cecilia unless you want your eye poked out. It's Cilly."

The perfect name for you, Al thought, but not in a meanspirited way. He'd warmed to her quirkiness.

"I saw the police in the street, coming from the house," she said, before he even had a chance to say 'Glad to meet ya', Cilly.' "What's going on?"

"Ah, they jes' came by to make sure everythin' is hunky-dory before the wake and that no killers are gonna' show up."

She looked at him and said, "Firstly, you like to lie a lot. Secondly, you're a terrible liar, because I saw them carrying tons of boxes full of jars. Thirdly, aren't you going to offer me a drink?"

"No comment on the first two things. Yeah to the drink. Come with me." He led her into the living room, Louis trotting along behind them.

She picked out Bombay Sapphire gin and downed the glass in one swig. She grimaced, hunching her shoulders, then put out her glass for another drink.

"Hard day?" Al said, pouring her another shot. "Course ya' know Milton Arrowsmith. Why ain't ya' at the funeral?"

"Make it a double. Heck, a triple."

"Ya' sure?"

"Don't make me say it again," she said, but with a little smile. "Not a hard day, a hard month, a hard year. And I'm not at Milton's funeral because I felt too sick about the whole thing. I had to leave the church. Now, are you going to tell me that the police came in here with a search warrant to take away Philippa's herbal stuff because she made some kind of poison out of it, put it in the chocolate, and killed Milton?"

Despite the subject matter, Al chuckled. "Looks like I ain't gonna' have to."

"Well, two and two always makes four," she said breezily. "It makes perfect sense, too. Although I'll bet it was Jonty and Philippa working together." She kicked off her boots, sat down on the couch, and put her feet on it, making herself at home.

This stranger put him at ease. Al sank into the armchair next to her. "What makes ya' say that?"

Louis didn't jump up on Al this time, he jumped up on Cilly and started nuzzling into her. Al took that as a good sign. He'd always thought dogs were far better judges of character than people.

"Oh, hello, lovely Louis." She stroked his head gently and then looked at Al. "Stock in Milton's company was about to tank. He'd persuaded his friends to buy tons of shares in it, telling them it was about to rise like bread with too much yeast, and since they were his good friends, he wanted them to cash in.

"But he only did it to boost the share price, so he could sell his at a higher price, then get himself out of the financial mess he was in using the money he got from the stock sale. Once he got his money out, the company would tank, and his friends and investors would lose all their money." She shook her head.

"Some people are disgusting. Many of us have money worries, but we don't go out there scamming our good friends out of millions."

That was a bombshell for Al. His mind was already thinking of ways how he could verify her story. He didn't know the first thing about the stock market and how to interpret it. Maybe Jake could find someone to look into it for them.

Cilly continued, "So Jonty found out about this little plot when he inspected the financials after they'd already made their investment. He's so busy and so over-confident he just bought them on trust without really looking into it. They sold their shares back while they were still high, so they've made quite a bit of profit. And then they killed him for revenge."

"Hmm," Al said, sitting back in his chair. "That's quite a theory."

She rolled her eyes. "I just can't believe the police haven't found out about it yet."

"Why ain't ya' reported it?"

"And have them scrutinizing my personal business? And having to go on the stand at a trial and all of that? No way."

Al sat in silence for a few moments, then he asked, "How do ya' know all of this?"

She didn't answer.

"Cilly, how do ya' know all of this?" he repeated.

She didn't answer again. She was lying with her back to him, Louis curled up in her lap. Al, feeling concerned, got up, and saw her eyes were closed and her mouth was open. She looked very much like a dead body.

CHAPTER TEN

Al reached down and shook Cilly, and she immediately sat bolt upright, looking confused. Louis stood up as if on alert, saw that nothing was wrong, and curled up in her lap again. "Oh dear. I've done it again, haven't I? Fallen asleep. I'm terribly sorry, Al, but I suffer from insomnia, and I can't sleep at night. So I drop off to sleep in the most inconvenient places. Especially if I have a little alcohol."

"It's okay," he said with a relieved chuckle. "I thought maybe someone had poisoned ya'."

"You joke," she said, "but I'd keep an eye out on what you eat or drink tonight. Philippa and Jonty may well have another plan up their sleeve."

"Ya' seem pretty sure it's them," he said.

"Just you wait and see." She looked at her little gold watch, which looked to be quite expensive. "I expect everyone will be back soon. The church was utterly packed. Although Philippa mentioned only inviting our Group, I wonder if other people will get wind of the wake. They won't all fit in this house."

"Wow," Al said. "And this house is humungous. So there's an army of 'em at the funeral?"

"An army of fashionistas," Cilly said. "All there to be seen and photographed by the paparazzi, I have no doubt. You do remember that Milton was a famous fashion designer, don't you?"

"Paparazzi were at the funeral? Ya' don't think they'll end up here, do ya"?"

"Oh no!" Cilly said. "Philippa wouldn't stand for it at the best of times, and she certainly won't now. Imagine if one of them came and took a picture that gave the murderer away!

"I'm sure that's the only reason they're holding the wake. To throw suspicion off of them. I'd keep your eyes peeled, if I were you. She's a smarter woman than she appears, and as for Jonty? He's a genius. I'm sure they've come up with a very cunning plot to frame someone else."

Al didn't know what to believe. He listened to everything Cilly said, but the more she went on about it, the more sceptical he became. What was it about 'the lady doth protest too much'? Maybe Cilly had something to do with the murder and was trying to throw suspicion off of herself?

She gently eased Louis off her lap and walked over to the window. "Just like I thought. Cars are already arriving." She sighed and came over and shook Al's hand.

"It's been a delight talking to you, Al. However, this is probably the last time I'll speak to you today, because I don't want to be seen talking to you during the wake. My boyfriend is rather protective, and he doesn't like me talking about the murder. Anyway, I can't exactly share my theories with everyone, can I?"

"Not unless ya' wanna' be forced to leave the house if Philippa finds out what yer' thinkin'," he said with a grin. "Nice to meet ya, Cilly. Ya' brightened up my mornin'."

"Glad to have been of service," she said, with an eccentric little curtsy. "I'm going to try and locate some champagne. If I die, you'll know the champagne was poisoned." She laughed, and then she was gone.

Louis came and wrapped himself around Al's legs, while Al stood for a moment, wondering what to do next. Should he hole himself up in the security room where he could view all the goings on via the security cameras, like Philippa wanted him to do?

Or should he ignore her wishes and stay downstairs? Also, should he tell her the police had seized her collection of herbs?

There was no time for him to answer his own questions, because he heard the front door open. He went into the hallway and found Philippa, Jonty, a tall older man wearing a very expensive looking trench coat and light scarf, and a very glamorous younger woman, with blonde waves tumbling down her back.

Coming through the doorway behind them was another couple who looked to be in their mid-60s, and seemed out of place in their shabby funeral wear. They both looked somewhat unhealthy, as if a life of hardship had caught up with them, causing them to have wrinkled faces and stooped backs.

Philippa gave Al a hard look, which he ignored.

She sighed, then stooped down to pet Louis. "Hello, my dear boy. I suppose you should meet your grandparents."

Al looked over at the shabby couple.

Philippa scooped Louis up in her arms and took him over to them. "Meet your grandparents, Jean James and Uriel Arrowsmith," she said in a baby voice. "They live in Mexico. They've come as a… delightful surprise." The way she said it made it very plain she did not think it was delightful at all.

Uriel looked at the dog with contempt. "What kind of mop is that? Trust Milton to get such a ridiculous-looking thing."

Jean gave him a sly dig in the ribs.

"What?" Uriel protested loudly. "I didn't say nothin'!"

Al remembered back to something he'd learned from a course he and Jake had taken. It was about people who have murdered and try to cover it up. Their instructor had told them that killers always had something negative to say about their victims, and treated them with contempt. Innocent family members and friends usually forgot the issues they'd had with the deceased, and even idolized them.

"It's a psychological protective mechanism called 'justification'," the instructor had said. "To ward off their own guilt about the murder, they try to think as negatively as possible about the victim. Their contempt then shows in their facial expressions, body language, and the things they say."

It had stuck in Al's mind as they'd watched a video about a mother who had killed her own children, but pretended they'd been abducted. Whenever she spoke about her kids on TV interviews, her lips curled into contempt, and she gave accounts about their bedwetting and disobedience.

It was a chilling video to watch. Looking into that woman's eyes, and knowing she had shot and killed her own children, was something Al would never forget. And now he saw the same contempt coming from Uriel.

He wasn't about to take what Cilly had told him at face value, and mark the case as 'closed' in his mind.

No one knew that Milton Arrowsmith had any family. And now, here they were, having appeared from nowhere. Wasn't it just as plausible that they could have tracked down their now-successful son? Maybe they resented that he wouldn't share his wealth with them, so they killed him for it.

Without brothers and sisters or any children, Milton's money would probably go to them. Al remembered Philippa mentioned that

Milton's penthouse had been featured in a magazine. It would have been easy enough for someone to track him down from that.

Maybe the father killed him. Maybe the mother did. Maybe they worked together. They certainly had a motive. Al needed to find out when they'd arrived in Vancouver.

"How did ya' get up here?" he asked. "I came in from Seattle. Normally I'da taken an airplane, but this time I decided to go by train."

"Airplane?" Uriel said scornfully. "What? So we can go die right away? Don't you know the airlines crash those planes on purpose? When they've got an old plane they don't want anymore, they send it down so they can get the insurance money. Then they can buy a brand spanking new plane, but never mind all the lives that are lost."

Al was so surprised he almost laughed out loud. That was a conspiracy theory he'd never heard before, but he wanted to keep Uriel on his side, so he said, "Yeah, I've heard that. So ya' came by train, too?"

"What, so we can derail and never be seen or heard from again? My brother died in a train crash," Uriel said. "I'll never set foot on a train as long as I live. Not a bus, either. The only person I trust to drive me is me."

Al nodded. "Ya' drove all the way up from Mexico? That's a long way."

"I used to be a trucker," Uriel said with a superior air. "I can handle it."

"We stopped a few places on the way," Jean said meekly, barely making eye contact.

Philippa laughed. "Al, have you finished grilling these poor people about their preferred modes of transportation? Can I get you a drink, Uriel, Jean? How about you, Ron, Alexis? We have champagne, and…"

"Champagne?" Uriel said, screwing his nose up. "I can't stand that drink. If you ask me, it's for women and sissies"

Al wondered if Uriel was contemptuous about everything, not just his murdered son. It sure seemed that way.

"I'll have to be a sissy and have a champagne," Ron, the tall man with the scarf said, with a hearty laugh. He slapped Uriel on the back.

"So will I," Alexis, the blonde, said with a laugh.

Philippa looked at Uriel in such a condescending way it made Al feel annoyed. She spoke to him like he was a petulant child. "And what would you like, Uriel?"

"She'll have a champagne," he said, tossing his thumb at Jean. "Beer will do me."

"Okay," Philippa said. "We don't actually have any beer, but I'll send one of the catering staff to the store to get some for you."

"Catering staff?" he murmured with an eyeroll. "Okay."

Al was beginning to see why Milton hadn't been in communication with his parents. His father was completely repulsive, and his mother was meek as a mouse. Al couldn't imagine her standing up for her son, herself, or anyone else. She just took whatever Uriel dished out.

"I don't believe we've met," Ron said, stepping forward and shaking Al's hand. He had a round smiling face, and looked like a friendly old uncle. "I'm Ron McGuire. This is my wife, Alexis Berry-McGuire."

Alexis gave Al a very firm handshake and looked intently into his eyes. She was obviously a very strong woman, probably with a very high-powered career. He didn't even need to know what she did, it just emanated from her.

"I'm Al," he said. He saw Philippa looking nervously in his direction from the doorway. He hadn't had time to think up another cover story, so he said, "You'll have to excuse me fer jes' a moment," and went over to her. They walked down the corridor together to the kitchen.

"I thought I told you to be upstairs," she said.

"Well, I ain't," Al said. "It's better if I'm down here. I can watch body language, and see what's goin' on. Cilly stopped by, ya' know. Gave me a whole buncha' info 'bout who coulda' killed Milton. I woulda' missed out if I'd been upstairs."

"That Cilly!" Philippa said, throwing her hands up in the air. "Don't believe anything she tells you. She's a poet, so she's rather fanciful." She slowed down for a moment, sighed, and turned to him. She looked into his eyes, her own blue eyes filled with remorse.

"Look, Al. I know I'm not perfect. I'm far from it. I'm really sorry if I've treated you wrongly, or anyone wrongly. I'm just, I'm not quite myself at the moment."

Because you and your husband killed Milton Arrowsmith and weren't ready for the mental and emotional consequences? Al wondered.

"Honestly, Al, between you and me, I think I might be on the verge of a nervous breakdown." She came closer to him and whispered, "Have you found out anything about the affairs yet?"

"We've been purty busy with the security prep for the wake, ain't we?" he said. "But I'll try soon. I tried to get into his office, but it's locked."

She sighed. "It's always locked. He guards that key with his life, which makes me think he's hiding something."

She looked so real in that moment Al decided to tell her the truth.

"I don't wanna' add to yer' bad news," he said. "But the cops came here durin' the funeral with a search warrant. They cleaned out yer' herbal room. Took it all."

All of the color drained out of Philippa's face. "Why?"

"They wouldn't tell me."

"Why didn't you stop them?"

"I ain't a judge, Philippa, I'm jes' a PI. Can't override a search warrant issued by a judge."

She shook her head from side to side, looking down at the ground. "Of course you can't. I'm sorry."

"It's gotta' be somethin' to do with Milton's murder," Al said. "Herbs… poisons…"

"You don't think I…?" she said with a gasp.

"I think we gotta' jes' wait and see what the cops find," he said diplomatically. "And even if they find somethin', don't necessarily mean it was ya' that used it. Ima sure loadsa' people have access to that room…?"

"Yes, my husband, Beth, the cleaner, visitors," she said. "I don't lock it very often."

"Did ya' have any castor beans?" Al asked. "Milton Arrowsmith was killed with ricin concealed inside the chocolate. Ricin's made from castor beans."

"I did," Philippa said, as her eyes became wide. "I make castor oil. It's really very good for all sorts of ailments, both topically and by mouth. Do you suppose they'll think I'm guilty?"

"I dunno'," Al said. "Wouldn't think castor beans on their own would be enough to arrest ya'. If ya' had any of the equipment to make ricin, or had ricin itself, they might think differently."

"Oh, Al, I swear it wasn't me!"

"What's not you?" Alexis Berry-McGuire said as she powerwalked down the hallway towards them in her black patent high heels.

CHAPTER ELEVEN

Philippa laughed nervously as Alexis approached. "Oh, nothing. Just, well, it well, it doesn't matter."

Al noticed she wasn't a very good liar. Maybe she really didn't have anything to do with Milton Arrowsmith's murder. Who knew? It was too early to say.

"I came to escape Milton's parents," Alexis said. "Well, his father, really. No wonder Milton didn't have any contact with them. And I thought my parents were bad. Anyway, let's get some of that champagne. The more we get down our throats, the more bearable those people will be."

"They've just lost their son, Alexis," Philippa said quietly. "You could be a little more sensitive."

Alexis shrugged. "I never saw them come around while Milton was alive. They've probably come here for his inheritance. And it's likely they'll get it, too, unless he's left it all to Louis. I wonder if he had a will or a trust. Do you know, Philippa?"

"I don't," Philippa said, "and I don't think we should talk about it. Let's take some trays of champagne out to the guests. I tried to keep the wake quiet from the funeral-goers, but I'm still half-expecting an inundation from all of Vancouver. I spoke to a designer who had flown all the way from Hong Kong to be at the funeral, so I did invite him. It would have been rude not to."

While Philippa was talking, they walked down the hall and into the huge kitchen. A swarm of catering staff was plating hors d'oeuvres on platters.

"Ah, brilliant," Philippa said. She turned to Alexis proudly. "They make these from scratch on site. That's why I chose them."

"Right," Alexis said, like it was completely irrelevant to her.

Al couldn't quite get the gist of their interactions, but it seemed Philippa was trying to impress Alexis, and bring her down a peg or two at the same time. Maybe she was insecure, or Alexis intimidated her?

Philippa cornered a young waitress. "Send people out with the champagne." Then she took Al to the corner of the kitchen, away from Alexis. "I've changed my mind about you bringing out champagne. It will invite too much attention. I think you should go back to the security room."

"Donchya' think it'd be safer with me minglin'? That way, if anythin' kicks off, I'm right in the middlea' the action."

She cocked her head to one side. "True, true. All right, then. But please try to be as inconspicuous as you can." She looked at his height and bulk and said, "If you can manage it."

He couldn't figure out what her obsession was with wanting to hide him away?

He returned to the entrance hall with Louis at his heels and found that Philippa's prediction had been right. A lot more people had arrived, and the hallway was packed to the brim. He began ushering people through to the living room. "Come on through, come on through," he said. Before long, the waitstaff arrived offering the hors d'oeuvres on giant platters, and carrying glasses of champagne on trays.

Al took a glass of champagne and just one hors d'oeuvre. He considered getting one for Louis, but wasn't sure what Louis could or would eat. He didn't want to cause a reaction or poisoning. He wasn't exactly sure what was poisonous to dogs besides chocolate.

Al took a glug of champagne and popped the hors d'oeuvre into his mouth. It was some smoked salmon and cream cheese concoction, with a bunch of other flavors, none of which he cared for. Although Al was used to gourmet food, since his wife was a food critic and his partner's wife was a caterer, the salmon and cream cheese just didn't taste that good to him.

But in all honesty, he never did see what all the gourmet food fuss was about. He couldn't believe anyone would choose a dainty piece of pheasant when you could have a hearty Italian lasagne followed by a boozy tiramisu. In Al's mind, it was madness.

"My wake was better," Al mumbled to himself. He'd had to fake his own death a little while back to avoid some Mafia reprisals. Cassie had put on quite a spread, with all kinds of traditional rich Italian dishes, and he'd had the meal of his life once everyone but DeeDee and Jake had left. They'd protested it might be bad luck to eat your own funeral food, but superstition was never going to get in between him and a good authentic calzone.

Looking through the crowd, he spotted Cilly and her boyfriend. She was hanging on his every word and was very tactile, rubbing her hand over his chest, putting her other arm around his waist. At the same time, she and Alexis were whispering together.

Soon the man pulled her away, looking around, worry on his face. He was a tall, strikingly handsome man with tan skin, huge brown eyes, and black wavy hair falling past his shoulders, but he seemed quiet, not bold and brash like Jonty could be.

As he thought about Jonty, Al wondered where he'd gone. But there was no time to think about him right now. Guests were streaming in the front door, and Al wanted to get a sense of who had come to the wake. He wondered if, among all these supposed 'well-wishers', the killer lurked, enjoying the fact he or she was getting away with what they'd done?

Alexis' question about Milton's will or trust had triggered Al to wonder if Milton had a will or a trust. If so, who was the executor or trustee? It wouldn't have been either of his parents. Maybe it was one of the Group? Perhaps it was Jonty or Philippa?

While he knew a little about the laws governing when someone died without a will in the U.S., though it varied state by state, he had no knowledge of the process in Canada.

He quickly whipped out his smartphone and began searching.

"Ah," he said aloud.

When an individual dies without a will in Canada, family members may apply to the court to act as the estate administrator. They will then identify and settle all debts, then determine how the residue of the estate is to be divided between the legal heirs. The usual order of priority for inheritance is – spouse, then children, then parents, then brothers and sisters, then more distant family such as nephews and nieces.

Well, then, Al thought. *That's gotta' be why his parents are here.*

Sometimes he hated being a PI because it made him so cynical. Or maybe it was just more realistic. Between that and the Mafia, he'd met his share of very shady characters, but at least the ones in the Mafia made no pretence about being 'good guys'. They were criminals, and they knew it. But being a PI, he'd found more than enough despicable behavior and appalling motives among 'good, upstanding citizens' to last him a lifetime.

So it was easy for him to believe Milton's parents didn't care about their son, and that all they cared about was his money. Whether or not they had killed him was another matter, but they definitely had a motive.

To test this theory, Al needed to get his hands on two things. First, any information he could get about Uriel and Jean's whereabouts on the day of the murder, and second, the security camera footage from the hotel on the same day.

The first would have been easier to get if they'd taken a plane or train, because there would be records they could probably get access to. But driving? That was tougher. If they had a modern vehicle with a good PS navigation system, he could get into that. But Al had the distinct feeling they drove an old beat up car or something similar. It just 'fit' with them.

There were other things he wanted to check out, like Jonty's office, for one.

He made up his mind as soon as he could, he'd start looking for all these things. He noted them down on his and Jake's special diagram, then he put his phone away, and decided to start talking to people. Maybe he'd pick up some clues along the way. But then he heard angry shouting, and ran through the crowd toward the source of the noise.

A young man in a cheap suit was pushing Uriel, yelling in his face. And Uriel, despite looking pretty decrepit, was holding his own, his strong, wiry arms lashing out at the young man.

Al got in the middle of them and pushed them apart. "No fightin' in here!" he bellowed. "Now, tell me what in the heck is goin' on here!"

CHAPTER TWELVE

The young man lunged at Uriel, angry tears streaming down his face, but Al's bulk blocked him. "He just called me a bastard, and said I ain't his family!" he cried, his face red.

He was a muscular young man with a couple of tattoos and a close-cropped haircut. He reminded Al of the youngsters in the Mafia, the youngster he had once been.

"That l'il thug ain't no family of mine!" Uriel said. "I don't care if he says he's Milton's seed, I don't want anything to do with him."

Everyone gasped.

"Milton has a child?" Alexis Berry-McGuire said. "What the... Did anyone know about this?"

"Probably not," the young man said, wiping his tears away angrily with the back of his sleeve. "He wanted to hide me 'cause I wasn't good enough for his flashy life style."

"Come along, dear, let's go and calm down in the kitchen," Philippa said, putting her arm around him. She clearly wanted to avoid a scene.

"No!" he said, shaking her off. "I'm not hiding in some kitchen.

I'm not hiding anywhere anymore. My mom told me I didn't have a dad all these years, but on her death bed she told me about him, and told me he didn't ever want to see me. He never paid nothing for me!

"I grew up with roaches crawling over my bed while he has this penthouse that could have paid for more than ten houses, maybe even twenty. I'm here, and I'm here for the money. It ain't no secret. I deserve it."

He pointed his finger at Uriel. "You better not try and get a penny from me, old man. My mom told me all about you, even showed me a picture. You were ugly twenty years ago, and now you're old and ugly. She said you were horrible to her. And any person who's horrible to my mom's going to pay. Trust me."

"I don't even know your harlot of a mother," Uriel spat at him. "So crawl back into whatever hole you came from and leave us alone."

"Don't you worry," the young man said, narrowing his eyes. "Soon as I get my hands on the money, I'm outta' here. Now, who do I gotta' speak to about that? I got all my documents. Birth certificate with that piece of trash's name on it. So when do I get to go to the bank and get the money that's owed to me?"

"I'm sure Milton would have wanted to leave all his money to the arts," Ron McGuire said. "He never mentioned he had a son. Not once."

"Yeah, well, like I said, I'm no one's dirty little secret no more," the young man said.

Philippa had gone very quiet, so much so, that in all the commotion, Al had forgotten she was even there. But then she spoke up, her voice little more than a squeak. When Al looked at her, she was very pale. "Jonty's the trustee of Milton's trust," she said.

Oh, really? Al thought. *Not even five minutes ago ya' said ya' had no idea.*

She avoided Al's gaze. "Let me go find him." She scurried away through the crowd of people.

"Okay," Al said, taking control of the situation. "Come with me. What's your name, son?"

"Trent Pinkney."

"Alright, Trent," Al said firmly. He towered above the young man, but tried not to be intimidating. "Let's jes' get away from this crowd. Jonty will wanna' talk to ya' somewhere quiet 'bout all this."

Trent looked at him with suspicion in his eyes, but allowed Al to lead the way out of the living room. They passed Philippa in the hall, and Al nodded towards a door at the end of the hallway. Philippa nodded back.

When they reached the end of the hallway, Al took one of the keys he had to every room on the ground floor of the house except Jonty's office, and unlocked the door to the 'formal sitting room,' as Philippa liked to call it.

It was where all the paintings had been, along with a great deal of antique furniture and was off limits for the wake. Al closed and locked the door behind them. The walls looked naked without the artwork that was usually on them.

It was only when Al sat down that he noticed Louis wasn't with him. He'd gotten used to the little dog trailing around after him wherever he went, kind of like a little shaggy shadow. Maybe Louis had gotten spooked by all the drama and had found a quiet corner where he could go and calm himself down. Penelope was locked in Philippa's bedroom with a lot of food. Philippa loved the little Bichon Frise so much she didn't want to risk her getting trampled on during the wake.

"Wanna' take a seat?" Al offered.

"Nope," Trent said, shoving his hands in his pockets. "And don't start talking to me about nothing. I don't wanna' talk. I just want my money and to get outta' here."

"Be real careful talkin' like that 'bout it," Al said. "People could think you killed him for the money."

"No!"

"Found out 'bout it from yer' mom, it filled ya' with rage, ya' came here, poisoned him, and now yer' fixin' to get his money and split. Ain't lookin' good fer ya', Trent."

"I didn't kill him," Trent said, looking a little panicked. "If I woulda', I'd have every right to. But I didn't. Look. I can show you." He took his phone out of his pocket. "Look at this," he said, walking over to Al. "That's my flight from California this morning."

Al paused. "You coulda' flown back and forth again," he said. "It don't prove nothin'."

Trent started yelling. "I didn't kill my dumb father, a'right? Just get off my back, man. Jeez. Who the heck are you, anyway? The darn police?"

"Nah," Al said. "Jes' a friend of the family."

"Keep your nose out of it. And shut up 'til that guy gets here. I don't wanna talk to you."

Al kept quiet, but he watched Trent's body language as he moved around the room. Trent was determined to avoid eye contact or even look in Al's direction.

In a few moments, Philippa and Jonty arrived.

Jonty had a glass in his hand, not of champagne, but of some dark liquor with crushed ice in the bottom. He staggered as he stepped into the room, lost his footing, and almost fell flat on his face. His eyes were bloodshot and hooded.

How on earth could he be he drunk already? Al wondered. *They hadn't been back at the house for very long. He must have snuck a flask into the funeral. Or maybe it was Philippa who'd done the sneaking... sneaking some potent herb into his drink.* Al wondered if he was getting paranoid.

"You say you're... you're... his son. Whose son again? Oh yes, Milton's."

Trent stared at him in disgust. "You're drunk."

"Be quiet," Jonty slurred. "Right, so, where was I?" He sat down on one of the antique chaise lounges. "My condolences about your, about Milton," he said, slurring. "Well, since you're..."

"Jonty," Philippa interrupted meekly. "Don't you think we should do this another time? You don't sound very well."

He didn't say anything. He just held his hand up dismissively and went on talking to Trent. "Of course it was probably very easy for you to find..."

"Just tell me how I'm getting my money," Trent said, interrupting him.

"Papers. Papers. A lot of papers."

"Paperwork? Yeah, I got everything to prove it." He reached into his cheap suit jacket and produced an overstuffed envelope. "Look. Birth certificate. My mom's death certificate. What else ya' need?"

"A long stick," Jonty said, then there was a long silence while everyone wondered what he was talking about. He began to chuckle unsteadily. "To keep away all the gold-digging women. They'll swarm around you like bees or is it flies?

"Then you'll get trapped into marrying one, and you won't be able to get divorced because she'd clean you out and you'd lose your... your house." He laughed, then turned back to Philippa. "Isn't that right... darling?"

"I don't know what you're talking about," she said tightly. "And you're drunk, Jonty. I think you should go to bed."

"Bed?" Jonty said. "Listen, my boy, forget about the money. It never brought anyone happiness. It just complicates and corrupts even the purest things. Go home and forget about all of this."

Trent's voice wavered. "I want my money," he said, but he didn't seem quite as sure.

"Your funeral," Jonty said, then swigged back the last of the contents of his glass. "First Milton's, then yours." He laughed.

Al felt a chill running down his spine.

Was that jes' a drunken joke, Al wondered, *or did it mean somethin' more sinister? Maybe Jonty, as the trustee of Milton's trust, wanted all the money fer himself. Would he be prepared to kill Trent to get his hands on the money? But what about Milton's parents?*

Al realized Jonty hadn't been in the room, so he probably didn't even know they were here.

"Milton's parents are here," Al said. "Would they get any inheritance?"

"Are they?" Jonty asked, looking around, as if they were in the room. He looked back at Philippa. "Why didn't you tell me?" he exclaimed angrily.

Al looked at Philippa. All the color was still drained from her face. Why had she lied to Alexis about not knowing anything regarding Milton's trust? The pair of them were looking more and more suspicious by the minute.

"Look, boy," Jonty said roughly to Trent. "If you're stupid enough to want all this money, be my guest. We'll sign the papers tomorrow afternoon. Meet me here at the house at 2:00 p.m." He staggered to his feet and started to leave the room, clutching his head. "Little men... with pickaxes... inside my... head."

He fell against the doorframe as he tried to leave the room.

Al rushed to help him up. "I think ya' really need to get to bed."

Jonty laughed. "In the arms of a strong man, like you."

"Jonty!" Philippa said. "Oh goodness, Al, I'm so sorry."

"I've seen much worse," Al said simply. "Can ya' show me the way to yer' bedroom?"

"Sure," Philippa said. She leaned back inside the room. "You, out," she said to Trent.

"I'm outta' here. I'm comin' back tomorrow afternoon to sign the papers," he said.

"Fine," Philippa said tersely. She locked the door behind him, then unlocked another door further down the corridor which Al had assumed was a closet of some kind. It led to another, much smaller, staircase.

"I ain't seen this before!" Al said.

"We don't use it very often," Philippa said. "But I can't bear everyone to see him like this."

"See me like what?" Jonty spouted. "Telling the truth for once?"

Al wished Philippa wasn't there, so he could grill Jonty while he was drunk. It was the most talkative he'd seen him, and like Jonty himself had alluded to, *in vino veritas,* the truth always comes out after a bit of alcohol. Perhaps Al would be able to wiggle some information out of him.

"I'm so sorry, Al," Philippa said. "Really I am, for everything. My life is such a mess, and I've just invited you into all of it."

"I'm paying him enough for the privilege," Jonty said, laughing. "He's a tough fellow, aren't you, Al?"

"That I am."

"Philippa, did you know that Al was in the Mafia?"

Al's blood ran cold. How on earth did Jonty know that?

"W...what?" Philippa said.

"Yes! In Chicago," Jonty said. "I could run my own PI firm, couldn't I, Al? Don't worry, I won't hold it against you. We all have our dark and dirty secrets. Some are darker and dirtier than others."

"Stop talking," Philippa hissed at him. "You're not making any sense."

"Oh, but I am," Jonty said as they reached the top of the stairs. "I'm making the most sense of all."

"How did ya' know I was in the Mafia, Jonty?" Al asked.

Jonty laughed and tapped the side of his nose. "I have my ways."

He stumbled again, and Al managed to catch him just before he fell on the floor. "Did ya' know about Trent before he came, then? Ya' didn't seem all that surprised to see him."

"Of course I did!" he said. "I jes' know how to keep my mouth shut."

It was very ironic he should say such a thing, because, at that moment, his mouth opened, and he threw up all over the floor, and Al's black suede shoes.

"Jonty!" Philippa exclaimed. "Al, really, I'm so, so, so sorry."

CHAPTER THIRTEEN

Al put his suede shoes under the shower in his suite and picked out another pair. He was known for keeping it all together under pressure, and this was true now. He didn't feel rattled by any of the day's events, but so many theories twisted themselves up in knots in his head that he was starting to develop a headache.

Thankfully he had little Louis for company. He'd tracked Al down as he made his way back to his room. The poor little Barbet looked nervous and skittish, and yelped with relief when he saw Al. He was looking up at Al with curiosity on his face, wondering what was going on.

"Everythin's different now, pal," Al said, ruffling his neck after he sat down on the edge of the bed. "Yer' life's been turned upside down these past few days, huh? Looks like you'll have to get used to yer' new environment." He took a glance at his vomit-stained shoes that he'd removed from the shower.

"Can't say I blame ya' fer not bein' happy 'bout it," he mumbled. "But I'm gonna' find out what happened to yer master. Ya' can trust me on that one, pal. That's the least I can do for ya', hey?"

Louis climbed up into Al's lap and snuggled down against his bulk.

"Ah, ya' big softie," Al said with a smile. "We'd better get back out there so we can find out whodunnit." He gave Louis a quick hug, then eased him off his lap. "Right now Ima gonna' go put on my other pair of shoes. Looks like these ones will be goin' to the dry cleaners or put in the trash."

Quite unexpectedly, a memory of his grandmother came to mind. His *nonna* used to love all her authentic Italian phrases, and she'd often say *fare le scarpe a qualcuno*, which meant pulling the rug out from under someone's feet.

But what made him think of it was its literal translation 'to make shoes for someone.' It looked like Philippa and Jonty were taking shoes from him, and pulling the rug out from under his feet. His head reeled when he thought of all the details.

He was getting hungry, too. He looked at his watch. "Comin' up to 1:30," he said. "Gotta' be lunchtime soon. Louis, let's hope those caterers will lay on somethin' half-decent. I can't be doin' with no escargot or truffles or stinkin' cheese right now. I gotta' fill my belly with somethin' proper."

Thankfully, he was in luck. By the time he'd laced up his other shoes, patent black oxfords to go with his suit, and walked downstairs, he found the hallway and the living room empty and quiet.

"It's either the apocalypse or everyone's chowin' down," he said to Louis.

They headed to the dining room and found it was the latter. Someone had opened the double doors from the dining room that led onto the small yard at the back of the house, and people were out there eating and talking quietly. Finally, it looked and sounded like a regular wake, instead of a television soap opera.

Al looked over at the long catering tables and wrinkled his nose. "Here goes nothin', boy," he said, picking up a plate. "I'll keep an eye out for some steak fer ya'."

There were a few entrees to choose from, and a number of salads. There was also ciabatta and rosemary focaccia bread, Al's favorites, which he loaded his plate up with.

There was a seafood linguini, not one of Al's favorites, and some strange-looking dish he'd never seen before. It was a collection of shells, broken open and stuffed with something he couldn't quite identify.

He looked up and saw one of the catering staff hovering by the table.

"Can ya' tell me what this is?" Al asked him.

"Coquilles St. Jacques," the man said in a friendly tone. "It's mashed potatoes, scallops and Gruyere cheese."

"Ah, right," Al said. "Thanks." *More seafood? No thanks.*

But the final dish was a surprise and a delight.

"That's authentic Thai Weeping Tiger beef," the waiter said, watching Al look at it. "*Seau rong hai,* it's called. Sirloin beef steaks on a bed of sautéed vegetables, topped with grilled rice and Weeping Tiger sauce."

Al grinned. "I take it there's no actual tiger."

"Ha, no," the waiter said. "Soy sauce, fish sauce, and too many other ingredients to mention. If you like beef, that's the one I'd recommend."

"That I do," Al said, as he helped himself to a generous serving. He nodded down at Louis. "So does this l'il guy, but that sauce sounds like it'll blow his head clean off. Ya' got any plain steak strips for him? He's the dog of the man that died, ya' know."

"I'm not sure we do, but I'll go check in the kitchen for him."

"I'll come with ya'," Al said. "I need to look for a dog bowl. Don't think Mrs. Murdoch would be happy with me throwin' steak strips fer him to jump up and catch."

The waiter smiled politely, and they set off for the kitchen. Just before they got to the kitchen door, Al saw a man standing near it eating by himself. He smiled at Al and Louis and continued to eat.

Al didn't pay much attention to him and went inside the kitchen with the waiter. It was a hub of activity with the catering staff buzzing around like worker bees in a hive.

"You might not want to enter the fray," the waiter said with a laugh. "Let me see what I can find, dog bowl included."

"Thanks," Al said. It was so hot in the kitchen, sweat had already jumped out on his forehead. "I'll jes' be outside the door."

"Good idea."

Al walked out of the kitchen with Louis at his heels and breathed a sigh of relief. The man in the hall turned around and nodded shyly at Al, then resumed eating.

"Don't feel like bravin' the dinin' room?" Al asked with a grin. "Can't say that I blame ya'." Then he began to eat his Weeping Tiger sirloin strips. The sauce was out of this world. "Man, this Weeping Tiger thing is good."

"Hmm," the man replied.

But Al wasn't deterred by the man's lack of interest. "I'm Al De Duco, a friend of Philippa's."

That caught the man's attention. He whirled around. "She's never introduced me to you before. I'm Paul Spears."

"Ima new friend," Al said.

Paul looked at him and said, "You're not a PI, are you?"

"Why'dya ask?"

"Philippa told me she was going to get one," he said. "To make sure her security was top-notch, and, well, are you?"

"And to see if Jonty was having an affair," Al finished for him.

"Yes, but I didn't want to say that, in case you weren't." He came across as being pretty awkward.

"Do ya' think he is?" Al asked.

"I don't have any evidence," Paul said. He breathed in and out heavily, and was silent for a long moment, staring down at his plate. "But you don't need evidence to see that he's not a good man."

"Who is a good man?" Al said. "Show me one and I'll give ya' a million bucks."

"That's a rather cynical thing to say."

Al shrugged. "Bein' a PI" – *and in the Mafia* – "gets ya' that way sometimes."

"I understand somewhat," he said. "I'm an actuary, which makes me rather sceptical and pessimistic. But I've met enough good people not to be cynical."

"I guess I have, too," Al said, thinking of Cassie, Jake, and DeeDee. The environment in this household was getting to him. "A lot of actuaries work fer insurance companies, right?"

"Yes, and I do. In life insurance."

"Ah," Al said. "Seen any murders fer inheritance in yer' career?"

"Well, so-called 'slayer statutes' legally prevent murderers from inheriting from their victims, but obviously that only works if they get caught. Around forty percent of murders aren't solved, so I'm sure we've had some murders slip through the cracks that no one is aware of.

"And obviously there will be murders where the police have listed the cause of death differently, like if the killer has been very clever at making it look like a heart attack or something else, and of course we don't know those figures. But we can assume that the figure of unsolved murders is higher than forty percent. We just don't quite know how high it is."

"Yeah," Al said. "Speakin' of which, what 'bout the poison in the chocolates for Milton. Interestin' method to kill someone, huh?"

Paul went very pale. "I wouldn't call it interesting. I'd call it heinous. That's not a crime of passion. That's a carefully thought-out murder."

"You close to Philippa?"

He nodded.

"Then you know she has all those herbs she makes stuff outta' includin' castor beans, the base material used to make ricin. Ya' didn't suspect it was her?"

Paul looked like he was about to be sick. "No," he said, but didn't look convincing. "Why would you say that? Why would she want to kill Milton? She didn't have any reason to. And even if she did, she would never kill anyone. She's a lovely, kind woman.

"Yes, she gets overwhelmed sometimes, but that's only because she's so sensitive. She wouldn't kill someone. She couldn't. She's too gentle. She's too much of a good soul. Honestly, she's just not the type at all. It doesn't fit her personality profile. Remember, I'm an actuary. My job is to assess risk and probabilities. The risk of Philippa committing murder is so small it's negligible."

Al smiled at him. "Ya' like her a lot, huh?"

"She's my good friend," Paul said tightly.

Al could tell Paul was in love with her. It was painfully obvious with the way he'd rushed to her defense and the look in his eyes when he spoke about her. Al had no doubt he'd walk the whole world over for her.

Al was considering telling him about her herbal collection being seized by the police, but he didn't. It wasn't his place to tell.

"Well, it coulda' been anyone with access to her herbs," Al said.

"Or someone trying to frame her," Paul said. "You can buy castor beans all over the internet. People grow them. It could be someone who knows she has them, and wants people to believe it's her, when it's not."

"Gotcha'," Al said.

"But it would have to be someone who's pretty confident with working with their hands," he said. "Making ricin is a very dangerous job. I immediately researched it when I heard about it on the news. One can easily poison themselves during the process of turning the beans into ricin. I'd never dare attempt it for fear of poisoning myself. Doing something that requires that degree of detailed handiwork is definitely not my specialty."

"I see," Al said.

Just then the waiter came out through the kitchen door behind Al with a dog bowl filled to the brim with strips of steak. "Here you go," he said. "Sorry I took so long. It took forever to track down a dog bowl."

"Better late than never," Al said with a smile, putting his fork on his plate and using his free hand to take the bowl. He put it by his feet. "Thanks." Louis rushed to the bowl and began to eat. "See?

This l'il guy's enjoyin' hisself already."

The waiter nodded, smiled, then left.

"So," Al said, turning back to Paul. "Ya' got any idea who coulda' done this? Killed Milton?"

Paul shook his head. "I wouldn't…"

He paused as they heard a hard banging on the front door. That kind of banging never meant good news, and, in a physical reaction Al still hadn't managed to get rid of since his Mafia days, his palms started to sweat. Way back when, that sort of knock meant either enemies or cops.

They were the closest ones to the front door, so Al went to answer it.

It was two of the cops who had been there previously. One of them shoved a paper in his face again, and it felt like a very unpleasant déjà vu.

"Is Philippa Murdoch here?" one of them asked, exactly as they'd done before. Al would have thought he was in some kind of a time warp, except for the fact that he saw the words *ARREST WARRANT* in large capital letters at the top of the piece of paper the officer had handed him.

"Ye…yes," he said.

CHAPTER FOURTEEN

Al tossed and turned in bed that night, unable to sleep. Once Philippa had been arrested, 'on suspicion of first-degree murder,' Al had to get everyone out of the house, which had taken forever.

The worst of them all had been Uriel, who had yelled after Philippa, "You killed my son! You killed my son!" as she was being led away by the police, quietly crying. Uriel picked up an antique vase and smashed it on the floor of the hallway, then picked up the mirror by the door, and smashed that, too.

Al had to manhandle him out the door, and then clean up the mess of shards in the hallway, so no one would get hurt by stepping on them. Of course, Jonty was drunk in bed and not fit for any kind of managing, so Al had to make sure the caterers and the rest of the staff left, as well as all the guests.

It seemed to take a lifetime while they cleared up all the food, did the cleaning up, and loaded all their equipment into their vans, while Al had to stick around to make sure everything happened smoothly. All he wanted to do was retreat to his bedroom for a long hot shower and some serious thinking time. It had been a very intense day, to say the least.

But now, once everything was over, he'd eaten another delicious portion of Weeping Tiger beef, taken the long-awaited hot shower, and he was in bed under a nice warm comforter, Louis gently snoring by the side of the bed. He found he couldn't get a wink of sleep.

Al couldn't remember the last time he'd had such an intense day, either through work or in his personal life. He wanted to call both Jake and Cassie to share everything with them, but his thoughts were traveling around so fast in his head, he was having trouble making sense of them.

Philippa arrested.

Of course, that was the big news. But Al had been around police long enough to know they often got it wrong.

He wondered if they had new information, or if it was as a result of the investigation into her herbal collection. If it was the latter, they'd worked remarkably fast.

Finding it impossible to unwind and get to sleep, he decided watching a comedy on Netflix might help smooth out his thoughts and help him get to sleep. He was wired, like he'd drunk ten cups of coffee that day, when in reality, he'd only had one and it had been early in the morning. He knew it wasn't a good idea for him to stay up until the early hours of the morning, thinking. The only thing he'd accomplish would be to tie himself up further in knots.

But just when he'd decided to watch a stand-up comedy show, the house telephone rang. It was right next to his room on the landing. He jumped up and rushed out of the room, wearing only his boxers, to grab it from the cradle.

"Hello?" he said.

"Al? It's me, Philippa," she said, her voice so thick with tears he could barely understand her.

"Ya' got an attorney?" he immediately asked.

"Yes," she said, snivelling. "He's coming tomorrow. Is Penelope okay? Where is she?"

Al wasn't sure, but since she sounded so distressed, he told a little white lie. "I think I saw her goin' in yer' bedroom." He made a mental note to find her once the call had ended. With everything that had gone on, he'd forgotten all about her.

"Oh no! Don't let her stay on the bed! Jonty might roll over and crush her."

"Okay," Al said. "I'll go get her and bring her in with me and Louis."

"Yes, and make sure she's not hungry." Her voice broke. "My poor little girl."

"Don't worry," Al said. "I'll take care of her. B'sides, you need to be thinkin' about yerself for now."

"I didn't do it, Al! I didn't! I swear I didn't!"

"Okay," Al said. Thoughts of what Cilly had told him circled around in his mind. There wasn't much else to say. Right now, he had no clue if Philippa was innocent or guilty.

She heaved a great sob at the other end of the line. "You don't believe me, do you?"

"I jes' don't know, Philippa," he said. "Did ya' get any info on why ya' were arrested?"

"No," she said. "I don't even understand how all this works. Will I have to go to court for a trial with a jury and everything? I've never even thought about it before."

"Ya've been arrested because of their suspicion that ya've committee a crime," he explained. "They ain't charged ya' with nothin' yet. I dunno 'bout the laws in Canada exactly, but before long, probably in less than a day, they'll let ya' go, or if they charge ya', they'll take ya' to a judge for a bail hearing."

Philippa cried. "I just want to come home. I didn't do anything, really I didn't."

"Try to get some sleep," Al said. "Yer' attorney will be there in the mornin', and he'll tell ya' what to do. Do ya' know him well?"

"No," she wailed. "He helped Jonty out with something once, a business matter. I don't know him. I just remembered his name and got them to call him. Al, you're not a lawyer, are you? I'd feel a lot better with you here."

"I ain't," he said. If she was innocent, he really felt for her, but there was nothing he could do. "Do ya' want me to wake up Jonty and tell him what's going on? Do ya' wanna' talk to him?"

There was a pause, and Al heard a man's voice talking in the background. "I have to go, Al," Philippa said quickly. "Just tell Jonty to come see me tomorrow."

"Okay," Al said.

"Don't forget about Penelope."

"I won't."

Al was true to his word. He padded downstairs in his slippers to find Penelope cuddled up in the same armchair Philippa always sat in, sound asleep. He contemplated leaving her there, but in the end scooped her up.

He took both of the dogs outside in case they needed to do their business, and then brought them back up to his room. They curled up together, their paws crossing over one another, and in moments, had their eyes closed. He left his bedroom door open a crack, so he could hear the phone in case Philippa called again.

Al went back to his Netflix comedy show, and fell asleep halfway through it.

*****

The next thing Al knew, he was awakened by paws patting him on his face. He sat up with a jolt. Sunlight was streaming through the sheer curtains. "Looks late," he said to Louis, who had been the one pawing him. Penelope was nowhere to be seen.

He scrambled for his phone on the bed, and eventually found it. It was 10:30 a.m.

"Oh, man," he said.

He got up, threw on his robe, and went to Philippa and Jonty's bedroom to let Jonty know Philippa had been arrested, and that she wanted to see him. He knocked, but there was no answer.

"Jonty!" he called out. Nothing. "Jonty?"

He opened the door carefully, but there was no sign of Jonty. The bed hadn't been made, and Jonty's clothes from the previous night, which had vomit on them, were strewn across the floor.

"Jonty?" he said again, walking over to the bathroom. The door was open, but Jonty wasn't in there.

He hurried out of the room and went downstairs, calling out for Jonty again and again, louder each time. But the house was empty.

He called Jonty on his cell phone, but it went straight to voicemail.

"Great," Al said sarcastically. "Of my clients, one's in jail, and the other's gone AWOL. Swell."

Louis made a whining sound.

"Tell me 'bout it," Al said. "Oh, yer' hungry? Let me see what I can get ya'. And a coffee for me. Don't remember the last time I slept this late. And where's yer' lady friend, huh? I hope she ain't run away, too."

He turned on the coffee machine in the traditional classic kitchen, and looked in the refrigerator, hoping to find Louis' beef strips. "No luck, boy, sorry. Think yer' gonna have to get used to dog food."

He'd seen Philippa feed Penelope in a little side room off the kitchen especially maintained for that purpose. He squeezed out a pouch of the dog food and hoped Louis would be hungry enough to go for it. "It's still beef," Al said. "Go on, try it."

Louis sniffed it suspiciously, but then began to nibble at it.

"Atta' boy," Al said.

Penelope, who must have smelled the food from somewhere else in the house, came in and joined Louis for breakfast. Al squeezed out a pouch for her, and then another one for good measure.

"The two of ya' can have yerselves' a feast," Al said.

After he'd had his coffee and a quick shower, Al was ready to head out to the police station. He thought about taking the dogs along, but decided it was best to leave them home for practical reasons. He also considered getting that car he'd thought about renting, but since he was running late, he thought it better to get a cab. He called Jonty again on the way out, but it went to voicemail.

A short time later the taxi pulled up at the police station, which was obviously new, and painted in a fashionable steel gray. He marched right up to the front desk, ignoring the people sitting around and the man in a suit standing just to the side of the desk.

"I'm here to see Philippa Murdoch," he said, trying his luck.

The cop at the desk looked at him and cocked her head to one side. "I know you're not her attorney."

"How do ya' know that?"

"Because I am," the man in the suit said.

"I see," Al said. He moved around to the other side of the man, so he wasn't blocking access to the cop at the desk for anyone, and put his hand out. "I'm Al De Duco. Philippa hired me as a PI for various reasons. What's goin' on with her case?"

"Yes, she told me about you. Where's Jonty?"

"I dunno'," Al said. "He was gone when I woke up this mornin'. His phone's goin' to voicemail."

"I know, I've been trying it, too. Anyway, they've questioned her. They're going with the angle that she made the ricin from the castor beans and injected it into the chocolate."

"Ah," Al said. "How'd she do when they questioned her?"

"She was flustered. I told her to go with no comment the whole way through. I didn't get to see her afterwards, but I will in a moment. I'm waiting to go in there right now."

"It don't seem like a very strong case," Al said, "if that's all they got."

"Of course they need more evidence than the herbal collection," the attorney said. "And they have it. Her fingerprints were on the chocolate box."

"What did ya' say?"

"The chocolate box, they found traces of ricin in it, and…"

"Course her fingerprints are on it," Al said. "She and I found it at Milton's apartment and brought it over here."

"What?"

Al laughed at the absurdity of the situation. "Didn't they mention that when they were interrogatin' her? Didn't she react when they brought it up?"

The attorney looked very uncomfortable. "Well, she said, 'No comment,' like I'd told her to. She did give me a very meaningful look, but I thought she was just worried about the fact they had that evidence."

"What? I can't believe this," Al said, chuckling with relief. "She brought it in, and I was with her. How did they not know that?"

The attorney went over to the cop at the front desk. "Excuse me," he said. "I need to know some information about a piece of evidence that was brought in. It's relevant to my client's case."

The cop looked cooperative. "Okay. I'll do what I can."

"When was it?" the attorney asked Al.

"Um… Monday. At 'bout 3:00 p.m., I'd say."

The attorney relayed that information to the police officer, and a short time later she printed out a sheet of paper and handed it to him.

It had details about the chocolate box, but under the name of the person who brought it in, it said Al De Duco.

"They put my name in, and left hers out!" Al said. He scanned the paper. "Who was the person who checked it in? I 'member it was a man. Oh look, here it is, an Officer Taylor."

"Is Officer Taylor here?" the attorney asked the police officer.

"No," she said. "He doesn't work here anymore. His last day was Tuesday."

"Aha!" Al said. "There you have it. Look, all they gotta' do is…"

"Go watch the surveillance footage from when the chocolate box was brought in," the attorney said. "That's the explanation for her fingerprints, and then they've got no evidence to charge her or hold her. They'll have to release her immediately."

Al smiled. "Yep."

CHAPTER FIFTEEN

"I've half a mind to sue those bungling police idiots!" Philippa said, dusting off her expensive jacket like she was trying to get the jail off of it.

"I wouldn't be surprised if you got somethin' fer yer' time and trouble." Al said. "They basically held ya' fer no reason at all."

The three of them walked out of the police station and headed towards the parking lot.

"I'll give you a ride home," the attorney said.

"Thanks, Tom," Philippa said, then turned to Al. "Where's Jonty?"

"I dunno'," Al said. "He was gone when I got up this mornin', and his phone's off. Lemme' try him again." He did, but it went to voicemail. "Has he ever done anythin' like this before?"

"No," Philippa said, but as they got into the back of the attorney's car, she gave him a meaningful look as if to say *We'll have to talk later about this. Not in front of him.*

When they got home Louis and Penelope raced through the hallway to greet them. "Oh, my sweet girl," Philippa said, scooping

Penelope up into her arms and dotting her head with kisses. "Mommy missed you so, so much. Were you all right? Yes? Oh good."

Louis only briefly butted up against her ankles, then came straight for Al. "You're gettin' purty attached to me, huh?" Al said. "He's gonna' wanna' come home with me, this one is. Philippa, you were saying 'bout Jonty doin' somethin' like this before…"

"Yes, he's disappeared more than once before, and that's why I'm concerned about infidelity," she said, then paused. Her gaze landed on the phone, and a red light flashing on it, indicating a message. "Just a moment." She went over and pressed the button.

"Good morning. This is Nurse Melissa Frederick from Vancouver Coastal Hospital. I've tracked down this phone number as matching the home address of Jonathan Murdoch. I'm trying to reach Philippa Murdoch or a family member. Can you please call me back?" Then she gave the telephone number of the hospital.

"Oh no!" Philippa said, all in a panic. "Is he sick? What's going on? Oh, I can't remember the number. How do I replay this darn thing?"

Al had a head for numbers. "8-5-7-4-9-2-4."

Philippa punched the numbers in. "May I speak to Nurse…? Oh help me, my mind's gone blank."

"Melissa Frederick," Al said.

"Melissa Frederick," Philippa repeated.

She waited, the phone to her ear. "They're putting me through," she whispered to Al. "Come on, come on, come on, hurry up. … Yes, hello. It's Philippa Murdoch here. You left a message for me about my husband Jonathan… Unconscious?… Yes, I'll be there as soon as I can."

She slammed down the phone. "Let's go, Al. Jonty's unconscious! Call a cab, quick, we've got to hurry. Oh no… this is going from bad to worse. Just one thing after another!"

A little later, Al and Philippa stood quietly next to a hospital bed looking at Jonty's motionless body.

"My goodness," Philippa whispered under her breath. "What on earth is happening?"

The doctor had just left the room, having told them they weren't sure what was going on at this stage, only that they had taken some blood and had sent it to the lab for tests. "The results should be back in a few hours," he'd said.

Al shook his head, looking down at Jonty. "Wonder how this happened. They said he was found on the street at 'bout 11:00 a.m., which was jes' after I left the house, then he was brought in here about 11:30 a.m."

"I guess we won't know until he wakes up."

If he wakes up, Al wanted to say, but he held his tongue. He wondered if Jonty had been poisoned like Milton, and this was just the beginning of all his organs shutting down.

"Jonty?" Philippa tried, speaking loudly. "Jonty? Wake up! I'm here to see you with Al!" But Jonty remained still, his eyes shut, his face looking pale and lifeless.

Al didn't think anything was going to be accomplished by the pair of them standing there staring at him, and besides, he was getting hungry, having had no breakfast and now it was lunchtime. "I'm gonna' go grab a sandwich or somethin' in the cafeteria, Philippa. Do ya' want anythin'?"

She sighed. "I suppose I should eat something, but it seems so wrong to eat while Jonty's… like this."

"I know," Al said. "But it won't do no one no good to have low blood sugar."

"True."

"What 'bout a coffee with sugar or somethin'?"

"That would do nicely," Philippa said. "And some kind of cheese sandwich, if they have any, Al. Here…" She opened her purse to get out some money.

"Ima gettin' it," Al said.

He returned with two sweet coffees, a cheese panini for Philippa, and a meatball sandwich for himself.

"Thank you ever so much," Philippa said.

At that moment, Jonty suddenly sat up and proceeded to throw up all over himself and the hospital bed.

"Jonty, you're awake!" Philippa said.

I've seen jes' about enough of ya' throwin' up to last a lifetime, Al thought, and grinned. He was glad Jonty had woken up, and he didn't have another murder on his hands.

He pushed the door open and yelled, "Nurse!" down the corridor. "He woke up! And he's sick to his stomach!"

He turned around and saw Jonty clutching his head. "What the… where am I? Philippa? Am I in the hospital?"

"Yes, you are, darling," Philippa said, going over to him and placing her hand on his arm, strategically avoiding where he'd thrown up. "You were unconscious. What happened?"

"I don't remember. My head is banging."

"I'll go get you some water," Al said, walking down the corridor, but the nurse had beaten him to it, and she quickly approached with a plastic cup filled to the brim.

She came in the room and handed it to Jonty, who drank deeply.

"Ahh," he said, with pure relief. "It's coming back to me now. My mind feels all foggy, but…" he said, realizing something. "The coffee on the table."

"What coffee on the table?" Philippa asked, panicked.

"Shhh," the nurse said soothingly. "Let's not have too much excitement. Talk quietly and calmly, please. Let's get that gown off of you, and I'll get you a new one." She helped him ease it off, and bundled it into a ball. Then she got a fresh one out of the closet and helped him into it. "How are you feeling?"

"I'm okay," Jonty said, but then he clutched his head and winced. "I have a horrible headache, though. Could I have some more water and an aspirin?"

"I'll get the water and check with the doctor about the aspirin," she said. "I just came on shift, and I need to check and see what the plan is for your treatment."

She left, and Jonty turned towards Philippa and Al.

"What happened, darling?" Philippa asked.

"Okay," Jonty answered. "I woke up at about 8:00 this morning, feeling okay, considering how much I'd had to drink yesterday. I couldn't find you or the dogs, so I assumed you'd gone out for a walk."

"She was…" Al began, but Philippa put her hand up for him to stop.

"Go on," she said to Jonty.

"I went downstairs, and there was a very nice-looking box on the side table in the hallway. I picked it up, looked it over, and saw it was a coffee sampler from a company called Adams. It had a few different testers of various coffees from all around the world. And there was a note on it, saying 'For Jonty.'

"I thought it must have been from one of the people at the wake, so I decided to indulge in some of *Ethiopia's finest blend,* according to the packet. I actually found it revolting. It tasted moldy, so I only drank a swallow or two, then poured the rest of it down the sink, and threw the sampler in the trash.

"Then I left the house, intending to go to the art dealer to bring some of the smaller paintings back home and discuss when they could deliver the larger ones.

"But just as I got out of the car, I collapsed in the street. I remember my phone smashing to the ground. The next thing I knew I woke up here, right now."

"My goodness," Philippa said.

Al was thinking about the box of coffee and back to the previous night. He was the last one to bed, having made sure all the catering staff had left. He tried to recall if he'd seen the box, but in all honesty, he wasn't sure. He'd been pretty impatient for everyone to leave, as well as tired and worn out, so he wasn't at his alert best.

"I think someone wanted to poison me," Jonty said wearily. "Maybe to steal my paintings. That's why Milton was killed, wasn't it? They wanted to get their hands on a painting. So maybe they knew I was moving the paintings. Maybe they planned to send someone to collect the paintings 'on my behalf'." He gasped. "Philippa, quick, call the art dealer right now. Check and make sure they're all still there."

Philippa quickly got out her phone and called the dealer. The nurse came back in to give Jonty his second glass of water while Philippa was on the phone.

"The doctor says the aspirin is fine," she said, handing him a tablet.

"Thanks," Jonty said briefly, distracted by the important phone call Philippa was making. He swallowed the aspirin, and the nurse left.

"He's going to the locker to see if they're all there," Philippa whispered to Jonty and Al. Finally, she breathed a sigh of relief. "Oh, thank goodness. Thank you, Terrence." She tapped her phone screen to end the call. "It's all fine."

Jonty frowned. "That's strange," he said. "I was sure that's what the motive would have been for hurting me."

"Or maybe it wasn't poison at all?" Philippa ventured. "You did say the coffee tasted moldy. Maybe it was the mold that did something to your body. Does mold cause poisoning?"

"Time to consult Dr. Google," Al said, pulling out his phone. He spoke as he typed. "*Is… moldy… coffee… poisonous…?* Aha! Yes." He read aloud, "*If coffee is stored improperly, it can produce mold, which in turn produces mycotoxins. These toxins can cause poisoning when ingested at sufficient levels.*"

"There you go," Philippa said with a triumphant nod. "No one's trying to kill you, Jonty."

"But…" Jonty shook his head. "But I only had one or two swallows. Surely that can't have caused this…? I do want to believe you, but it just seems too much of coincidence after what happened to our friend."

"You mentioned you told some people you were transporting the paintings," Al said. "Who?"

"Umm…. Let me think. It was right after we'd returned from the church. Some of us were standing around talking. I remember Cilly was there. How could anyone forget her ridiculous fortune-teller turban? Alexis was there, and I think Paul Spears might have been there, too." His mouth turned up into a little contemptuous sneer.

"Philippa's *little friend*." Philippa put her head down and ignored him. Al made a mental note to try to get to the bottom of that later, but for now, there were more pressing issues at hand.

"Cilly, Alexis, and Paul," Al said. "Okay." *Cilly did seem extremely anti-Jonty,* he thought, *and very intent on making Al suspect him as much as possible. Maybe she had something to do with it. As for Alexis and Paul? He didn't know enough about them yet.* "Did ya' recognize the handwritin'?"

"No," Jonty said. "I was trying to figure out if I recognized it. It had a lot of loops and swirls, and I noticed the R was capitalized, while the rest was not. Except for the J in front of my name, of course. But I expect whoever did it changed their handwriting as much as they could."

"Sometimes it can be picked up by handwritin' analysis," Al said. "There can be distinct hallmarks in someone's handwritin', even if they're tryin' to write differently."

Jonty sighed. "Oh, well that would have been good, except for the fact it's probably buried in a landfill right now. I put the trash out before I left, and the trash truck picks up today around noon."

"Oh, dear," Philippa said. "Anyway, I'm sure it was just old coffee. Maybe they'd had the box for a while in their 'gift drawer' and didn't think to check to see if had gone bad."

"Could be," Al said.

"Maybe…" Jonty said, though he didn't sound convinced. A couple of moments later, he said, "No. No. I'm sure there's something more to it."

"Don't say that," Philippa said, her fake brave smile gone and her voice shaking all of a sudden. "Don't. Why would anyone want to kill you, Jonty? You've done nothing wrong."

"Neither had Milton," Jonty said.

"You don't know that," Philippa shot back. "He didn't tell us everything about himself, did he? We didn't even know he had a son."

"Oh! His son!" Al said. "He was supposed to come over this afternoon to see you, Jonty, remember? He wanted to find out 'bout Milton's estate and what he needed to do to get it."

"Huh? I don't remem… Oh, yes, now I have a vague recollection of talking to some young man, but it's really quite vague. Could you go speak to him on my behalf and rearrange the meeting for tonight or tomorrow?"

"Tomorrow," Philippa said firmly. "You need your rest."

CHAPTER SIXTEEN

Al returned to the house on Philippa and Jonty's instructions, to find Trent screaming outside the front door.

"You better let me in!" he yelled. "Or I'm gonna' bomb this whole place!"

"Whoa, whoa, whoa!" Al said firmly after stepping out of the cab and approaching Trent.

Trent jumped, not expecting him to be there. "Oh, it's you. Where's that guy? The guy who's supposed to get me the money."

"He's in the hospital," Al said. "Know anything about it?"

"What? Are you saying I hurt him?"

Al gave him a stern look. "Well, yer' here talkin' 'bout bombs. Ya' don't really seem like a chilled-out kinda' guy."

"I just want what I'm entitled to, man! Is that too much to freaking ask? When's he gonna be out? Nah, which hospital?" He got out his phone.

"Ya' ain't goin' down there," Al said. "You'll have to come back tomorrow, when he's well and home."

"No! You're just saying that! In fact, he's probably here right now! You're the one who told me to come back today. That's what you said!"

Al sighed. "Jes' go back to yer' hotel and come back tomorrow. He'll be here."

"I don't have a hotel."

Al frowned. "Huh? So where did ya' stay last night?"

"I didn't really stay anywhere," he said, not meeting Al's gaze. "Not all of us have a bunch of money for fancy hotels and all that. I told you I didn't have nothing. That's why I'm here. To get something from my dumb father."

Al reached into his pocket, took out his wallet, and gave Trent $200 in Canadian money. "That'll get ya' a bed somewhere fer a coupla' nights or more, if ya' choose well. I ain't a lawyer, but I guarantee you'll need to be stickin' around for a coupla' days to fill out the paperwork and all. Ya' can't sleep outside at night."

"The weather's not too bad this time of year."

"It ain't jes' the weather," Al said. "Streets in pretty much any city ain't safe at night. Go git a roof over yer' head, sonny, and we'll catch ya' tomorrow."

"Thanks, man," Trent said, slipping the bills into his pocket. "Wish I'd had a dad like you."

Al gave him a pat on the back. "Go on."

"See you tomorrow," Trent said, running down the street.

Al went inside, feeling a little sad. Just $200 in Canadian money and the kid wished Al was his father? His bar was set real low. Louis and Penelope rushed up to him the moment he stepped in the house. "Hey, can't a guy get in the door first?" he asked with a laugh. He stooped down to pet them both. "Ya' guys."

"Oh, thank goodness you're here," Beth said, hurrying into the front hallway. "That guy was here hollering for the longest time. I was about to call the cops."

"Don't worry, he's harmless," Al said. "Jes' has a good bark on him."

Beth gave him a lopsided half-smile. "That's good to know. With everything that's going on around here, I can't help but be a bit paranoid."

"Yeah, I know what ya' mean," Al said. "And now Jonty."

"What happened to Jonty?"

Al explained the situation.

"My goodness," Beth said, holding her hand to her chest in shock. "Someone was directly targeting him. And they'd been in the house." She shuddered. "That's horrible. Absolutely horrible."

"I know," Al said. "I'm jes' glad we ain't got another murder on our hands, that's what. Spoke to the doctor before I left the hospital, and he said Jonty could be outta' there tonight, dependin' on the blood test results."

"If I were him, I think I'd stay in the hospital," Beth said. "Seems like it's a lot safer." She looked around, like there might be murderers hiding in the hallway, behind the heavy velvet curtains, or crouching behind a side table. "I'll just be glad when they've found the culprit."

Al decided not to relay the story about Philippa's detainment by the bungling cops. Beth had far too much to worry about already.

"Yep. Fer now, I'm gonna' have a look over what I know so far. See if I can come up with somethin'."

"Sure," she said. "Need anything? A coffee? Do you want me to fix you lunch?"

"Thanks, but I've already eaten, and I jes' had some coffee. I better wait a coupla' hours."

"Okay. Let me know if you need anything."

"Thanks, Beth. Yer' a gem."

Beth looked at the dogs. "Come on, you two rascals. Lunch time." They happily trotted off after her, and Al went upstairs to his room.

He got out his phone and looked at his mind map, but only became increasingly frustrated. He went downstairs, popped his head into the kitchen to let Beth know he was going out, and left the house.

Al looked at his phone and saw that there was a park nearby. He decided to walk there, knowing that often he was able to think and process things better when he was being active.

He called Jake to run through some ideas with him. "Hi, Al," Jake said.

"My man. How's it goin'?"

"I'm glad you called," Jake said. "The case I'm working on is boring me to tears. It involves some complicated tax paper trail I'm trying to figure out. I got in touch with the forensic accountant we use, but I need to understand some of it myself, and now I'm even more frustrated."

Al chuckled. "Hmm, well. A lot's been goin' on up here." He relayed the events of the past couple of days to Jake. "I ain't had a spare minute to even think about who killed Milton Arrowsmith. And it looks like we got another poisonin' on our hands to contend with, Jonty, though at least he stayed alive to tell the tale. Aw man, wait a minute…" He turned on his heel.

"What is it?"

"Jonty said he threw the coffee and the note in the trash and it would be in the landfill by now, but I wanna' check and see if it's still in the trash can."

"Good idea. Anyone else come to mind who might have a motive to kill Milton and harm Jonty? Do you think his poisoning was attempted murder?"

"Hmm, couldn't say," Al said. "He only drank a swallow or two of the coffee. Maybe he was jes' lucky, 'cuz if he'da downed the whole thing, he'd be in the morgue right now. Course it could jes' be bad coffee, but my gut's tellin' me it ain't. Gut's tellin' me it was attempted murder."

"I'd agree," Jake said.

"Now, in terms of a motive, Milton's son coulda' offed Milton in order to make a play for the inheritance. Trust me, he hates his father's guts. And Milton's parents didn't know nothin' about this grandkid of theirs, so they woulda' thought they could get their hands on the cash if they got rid of Milton.

"There's also the theft of the paintin' as well. Ya' know it was gonna' be in the auction, and it weren't Milton's, but I ain't heard a peep from the owner. I don't know what's goin' on with that. Oh, and Philippa tol' me she didn't know a darn thing about the inheritance, then, next thing I know, her hubby's the trustee of Milton's estate. I dunno', a lotta' things jes' ain't addin' up right now."

"Couldn't agree more. It sounds complicated."

Al huffed. "Tell me 'bout it." He got back to the house and located the trash can. With his height, he could see from a little distance that it was empty. "Nothin' doin' at the trash can."

But he walked up closer to it to make sure, and as he looked into it, he saw a slip of paper at the bottom of the trash can. *For Jonty,* it read. "Bingo! Freakin' bingo! I got it, Jake! Wait a sec."

He pocketed his phone and made an attempt to pull out the note. It was stuck to the bottom, and it tore a little when he tried to get it out. "Darn." He tried again and very gently eased it out.

"Yes," Al said, grinning from ear to ear. He got out his phone and took a picture of the note. "Jake, I'm sendin' ya' this, and I want ya' to get a handwritin' analysis done on it ASAP."

"Will do."

"Now, I know those tell ya' whether they think it's a man, woman, what age, blah blah, but hear this… I'm gonna' try and get some handwritin' samples, anyways. I'll get Philippa's, though she can't be the one, 'cause she was cooped up in jail."

"Get Jonty's," Jake said. "Just in case he poisoned himself, and it's all a ruse."

"Yep. Wouldn't be surprised by nothin' these days," Al said. "Onea' the other people that stands out is Alexis Berry-McGuire. She made a song and dance about the will and heard Jonty talk about transportin' the paintings.

"An' Paul, what's his name? Oh yeah, Paul Spears. He was there, too. And this Cilly woman. Plus, she was tellin' me it was Philippa and Jonty that done in Milton. She was a l'il too strong fer me, if ya' get my drift. She might jes' be our woman."

"It is likely to be a woman," Jake said. "You know, they say poison is a woman's weapon."

"I don't put too much stock in that," Al said. "Jes' a smart person's weapon, and women are generally smarter." He chuckled. "Don't tell me when it's been a woman killin' that it don't take twice as long to figure it out."

"Oh, I don't know about that." Jake said.

"I do!" Al heard DeeDee pipe up in the background. "You're on speakerphone, Al! And you're absolutely right!"

"Darn!" Al said. "If I'da known ya' was eavesdroppin', I'da never admitted that."

"Ha!" Jake said.

"Well, ain't got time to walk in the park now," Al said. "I got work to do. Check in with you later. Get the writin' guy on it like yesterday."

"You bet. Good luck, buddy."

Al went back inside the house and began searching the sitting room for either Jonty or Philippa's handwriting, looking over his shoulder now and then to check that Beth hadn't come in. He went through the magazines on the side table, and the books on the shelves. And soon he found some gold.

"Aha!" he said, taking out a coffee table book of English Country Homes, with lots of large pictures of grand residences and castles. There was a note inside the front which read: *Dear Philippa. I hope this will bring back fond memories of our trip to England. Yours affectionately, Jonty.* Then there was a date, *13th August, 1995.*

"Man, these people been married a long time," he muttered to himself. He snapped a picture of the note, but it was blurry, so he had to try again. This time it was perfect, and he sent it to Jake.

Now for Philippa.

He knew their bedroom was unlocked from when he'd gone in there looking for Jonty that morning. Even though it felt like he was trespassing, he went up their bedroom. He found a notebook by her side of the bed with different handwriting. "Perfect."

That got sent to Jake, too.

"Next… hmm…"

He considered who he should go see first, Alexis Berry-McGuire, Paul Spears, or Cilly. Paul Spears was eliminated first. Alexis had been too interested in the will. Cilly had been adamant, trying to pin it on Phillipa and Jonty. But even so, he liked Cilly, and found it difficult to picture her as the guilty party.

So he decided to start with Alexis Berry-McGuire.

He called Philippa to ask for her number, which she quickly gave him, and he memorized it.

"Any update on Jonty?" he asked.

"Yes," she said. "They said he had rohypnol in his system. It's usually a…"

"Date rape drug," he said, interrupting her. "Yeah, I've heard of it. Wow. Okay."

"I've got to go, Al. The doctor's come in again. See you later."

"See ya'."

Al did a quick search on his phone and Dr. Google confirmed that *Rohypnol, commonly known as a 'date-rape drug' is a tranquilizer. It is about ten times stronger than Valium.* "Sheesh."

But there was no time to think about that right now.

He called Alexis Berry-McGuire's office number, and explained to her assistant who he was.

"She says to come right away," the assistant said. "There's actually something she wanted to discuss with you."

Before he left for the offices of Icon X, Al decided it was time for him to get some wheels. He called a local rental car company and they delivered a car to him within half an hour. Using Google Maps, he determined the route that would take him to Icon X, and he was soon on his way.

CHAPTER SEVENTEEN

After a short drive, Al parked his rental car and walked into the offices of Icon X, which, to be honest, were a little disappointing. He'd done some more search engine investigations, and found out they made all sorts of high-end security devices which wouldn't have been out of place in a James Bond movie.

So to discover they operated out of a boring brick building in an industrial complex was a bit of an anti-climax. He'd had in his mind's eye a sleek, tall, angular building made of black glass, or clad with reflective panels, so you couldn't see inside. But it looked pretty normal and mundane from the outside.

He was even able to get into the reception area, because a friendly man who appeared to work there let Al walk in behind him after he'd flashed his key card at the door sensor. He didn't question Al, just smiled at him.

"Huh, so much for security," Al muttered to himself, then went up to the front desk. "Afternoon. I'm here to see Alexis Berry-McGuire. Name's Al De Duco. She free?"

"Hi, let me check for you." The woman made a few clicks on her computer and looked at the screen. "You came at the right time. She was out this morning."

"In that case, guess I was lucky," Al said.

"Let me call her." She tapped on her phone. "Her line's busy. Do you want to sit over there for a moment?" she asked, motioning towards several nearby chairs.

"Sure," Al said. "I gotta' make a call myself, anyways."

A few moments later, the woman at the front desk called him over. "She's free now. She's on the top floor in the office at the very back. Would you like me to show you?"

"Nah, it's okay, thanks," he said. "I'm big and ugly enough to manage findin' it, I'm sure."

She smiled at him. Please fill in your name and the time on this list." He did so, and she got a visitor's pass from under the desk. "Just sling this around your neck, sir, and you're good to go."

"Thanks."

After he got in the elevator, he saw that the top floor of the building was the fourth floor. It all looked pretty old fashioned, and the floor was a bit of a labyrinth, but he eventually made it to the door of Alexis' office which said 'Chief Financial Officer' on it. He gently knocked on the door.

It opened immediately. "Al," she said, like they were old friends.

"Hey, Alexis," he said, shaking her hand. "Good to see ya'. Better here than bein' at a wake, huh?"

"Come in, come in."

Her desk was extremely clean and organized. There was only one paper on it which she appeared to have been working on, since it had a blue highlighter on top of it. He looked over at it surreptitiously, but couldn't see any of her handwriting.

"I find it strange that you should call me," she said. "Would you like some coffee?"

"Yeah, please. Black, no sugar."

"Sure." She called her assistant and asked her to get it. "So, as I was saying. It's strange that you should call me, because I really wanted to get in touch with you."

"Yeah, that's what yer' assistant said. What's up?"

Alexis laughed as she leaned back in her black leather executive chair. He noticed that she looked very at home in this environment. Very much in control and confident. "You first."

Al had to think quickly. He didn't want to let on his real reason for wanting to see her. "Could ya' do me a favor?"

"Depends what it is," she said with a smile.

"Could you jes' write down the names of the people in yer' Group? Ya' know, the group that gets together for all this stuff? I jes' wanna' check I ain't missed anyone. Then I was thinkin', let's draw lines between 'em, so you can show me who's real pally with who."

"Oh, okay, sure, I can do that," she said.

She took out a piece of scrap paper and laid it on the table. She pushed it toward Al and gave him a pen. "Let's start with my husband and me. I'm Alexis Berry-McGuire, that's M, small C, Capital G…"

"It's better if ya' write it," Al said, pushing the paper back to her. "I'm in a hurry, and I ain't never been the best speller."

She looked at him for a long moment, like she wanted to say no, but couldn't find a good enough reason.

"Okay," she said. She wrote her name, and Al watched closely. To him, it looked like she was doing it in an unnatural way, like she was trying to manipulate her handwriting into something it usually wasn't. Her fingers were sweating, and she had to adjust her grip on the pen.

She wrote all the names of the members of the group in a circle on the piece of paper, then drew arrows connecting some of them in order to make an informal diagram.

"Thank ya'," he said.

"I'd say Milton was closest with Jonty and Philippa. He and Paul Spears used to be very tight, but then they had a falling out for some reason. I don't know the details, but all of a sudden they stopped talking to each other at events, when before, they'd been in each other's pockets."

"Interesting. Didn't people wonder 'bout that after Milton got hisself killed?"

"I imagine some of them did," Alexis said. "I thought of it in passing, but Paul's straight as an arrow. Really, he's the last person on earth I'd think would kill someone."

"People said that about all sorts of psychopath killers," Al said. "Sometimes it's them quiet ones."

"That's true," Alexis said. "But what do I know? I'm a CFO, not an investigator."

"Let me jes' take a picture of this," Al said, lining his camera up to take a photo of her diagram. "I don't like to carry paper these days."

"Oh, me neither," she said. "Digital's definitely the way of the future."

He took the picture and sent it over to Jake. "Thanks for helpin' me with that. So why did ya' wanna' get in touch with me?"

She paused for a moment, then let out a long breath. "I was going to go to the police about this, but my husband said it would be better not to. They've got a reputation for getting things wrong. And what happened with Philippa? Is she okay?"

"Yeah, she's been released by the police. A misunderstandin'," Al said.

"You can't let anyone know what I'm about to tell you," she said.

"My lips are sealed," he said as put his thumb and index finger in front of his mouth and turned them.

"Okay." She took out her phone. "Look, here's a picture Cilly sent me a few days ago, showing me an amazing fur coat she found in a thrift store." She showed it to Al.

"And?"

"Look at the background," she said.

The entire background of the picture was a mess. Cilly's house was clearly a huge mix of eclectic finds from everywhere.

Alexis hovered her perfectly-manicured finger just above the screen, indicating a group of paintings that were stacked against each other on the back wall.

"Look at the one in bubble wrap," she said. "You can see the black frame through it and the red piece of the painting, right?"

Al squinted, just about making it out. "Yep, I think so. Zoom in."

She did, but it didn't help much, as the picture appeared to have been taken either in the evening or early morning, and the light wasn't very good.

"That's the painting that was stolen from Milton's penthouse."

"No!"

"It is, I swear it," she said. "I didn't even notice it when she sent the picture to me a few days ago, but I was just flicking back through some pictures today, and noticed it." All the color was drained from her face. "I think she, she and her boyfriend, killed Milton."

After Al left Alexis' office, he headed for the Bellevue Pacific Rim Hotel. He was sure the police had combed through the hotel's surveillance footage, but then he questioned his own assumption. Who knew? Now he wanted to check it for himself.

Did Cilly or her boyfriend enter Milton's penthouse on that day, and, more crucially, leave with a painting? And who came to the penthouse with the chocolates that day? What about Milton's parents? Did they come to his penthouse? And what about his son?

He knew the hotel technically didn't have to give him access to the footage, even with his PI licence. From experience, he knew the hotel didn't even have to give it to the cops without a court order. It depended on how difficult they wanted to be, and how important they thought they were.

Given the size and the grandeur of the hotel, he imagined they might think they were too important to acquiesce to requests from anybody at all, even law enforcement.

But he couldn't have been more wrong.

And thankfully, Al had learned plenty about bluffing from his days in the Mafia.

He knew creeping around like a mouse was going to get him precisely nowhere, so he blazed in with total confidence. While the valet had taken his rental car to park it in the underground parking lot, he'd quickly researched the manager's name, and learned it was a man named Kiran Chong.

He strode into the Bellevue Pacific Rim Hotel and marched right up to the desk, cutting in front of the small line of people. "Excuse me," he said to the young man behind the desk. He flashed his PI licence in his face and used his sternest voice. "I'm from Investigative Associates, to see Kiran Chong about a crucial surveillance issue."

"Of course, sir," the man said, jumping to pick up the phone and call the manager. "Is he expecting you?"

"He needs to see me," Al said, avoiding the question.

The young man just nodded, then placed the call. Al's confidence had bowled him over. "He's coming out here to meet with you."

The manager seemed to be in a very good mood, or maybe it was just the 5-star customer service. Either way, he pumped Al's hand with both of his and smiled like he was an old friend. "Kiran Chong. What can I do for you, sir?"

Al weighed the situation and decided to go with honesty. "Al De Duco. I'm sure you're aware of the tragic death of Milton Arrowsmith."

"Of course. Although he didn't use the hotel facilities often, we all knew him and little Louis."

"I'm a private investigator who's been hired by some of his friends to find out what happened to him. I found out some new information today, and I wanna' look at the surveillance tapes. I know it might need to be court-approved, but…"

"No, no, it's fine," Mr. Chong said. "We've supplied footage to the police, but haven't heard anything further from them. Our security office has surveillance of Mr. Arrowsmith's personal floor. You can view it. We have nothing to hide. Believe me, we'd love more than anything for his killer to be brought to justice. Let me take you up to the office right now, Mr. De Duco."

CHAPTER EIGHTEEN

Al walked out of the Bellevue Pacific Rim Hotel with his heart thudding in his chest. He'd seen the painting thief on camera. It was Cilly, and the killer was someone else. Were they working together? That was the final piece of the puzzle he had to fit into place. He didn't want to jump into making any accusations before he had everything straightened out in his mind.

He knew exactly where he needed to go next, to Cilly's. He called Philippa again, and she gave him the address. He decided not to call ahead this time. He wanted to catch her by surprise, and hopefully with the painting.

He had to hang around while waiting for the valet to bring up his car, so he spent the time trying to calm down and not jump to conclusions. It was so easy to do when you felt you were onto something.

Was it simply a matter that Cilly had sent the killer to cover her tracks after the theft of the painting? But why were those two people working together? It didn't make sense. There had to be some secret connection he wasn't aware of.

When he was back in his rental car, he punched Cilly's address into the GPS. Her apartment building wasn't far away. When he got there, he thought it looked like an old warehouse that had been spruced up by developers. He found on-street parking, which he thought cost a fortune, and then ran up the stairs to get to her apartment, because there was no elevator.

He heard the sound of very unusual music coming from her apartment. It sounded like some kind of spiritual music, with gongs and pan flutes. Under other circumstances, it would have been quite soothing, but right then, knowing he was walking into the apartment of a very friendly thief and possible murder mastermind, it sounded eerie and ominous. But Al was no wallflower, so he knocked confidently.

"Who is it?" Cilly sang out. She didn't speak it, she literally sang it.

Al would have laughed if the situation weren't so serious. "It's Al De Duco."

"I'm coming," she sang again.

He shook his head at the madness of it all. She opened the door a moment later, and the music got considerably louder. She was wearing a floaty white dress with white flowers in her long, flowing hair, looking like a picture of bohemian innocence. But Al wasn't fooled.

"Hi," he said.

"Come in, come in," she continued to sing.

His phone beeped. "Jes' a moment," he said, then slipped it out of his pocket. It was a WhatsApp message from Jake. It had Alexis' diagram of the social group and the 'For Jonty' slip of paper. *IT'S A MATCH,* the text read.

What? Now Al was confused. That didn't work with his theory at all.

He looked up at Cilly, who was walking over to the music and turning it off. His head was spinning. Could three of them be working together? Surely not.

"What are you doing here?" she said with a broad smile. "Don't get me wrong, it's lovely to see you, but it's quite unexpected."

"Philippa sent me," Al said, lying on the spot. "I'm goin' home tomorrow, and she's throwin' me a dinner party tonight. I was supposed to give you a handwritten invite, but I dropped them all through a darn grate. Ya' wanna' come?"

"Oh, yes!" she said, clapping her hands. "That would be absolutely lovely. You already know I'm not exactly enamored with Philippa, but I'd be delighted to see you off."

I'm sure you would, he thought.

"So where is it?" she asked.

"Aww, man, I can't remember the name," he said. "Some fancy Italian place." *Might as well get a good meal thrown into the bargain,* he thought.

"Oh, probably Bianchi's on Adera Street. We've all been there a couple times."

"Yeah, yeah, that's ringin' a bell. That was probably it. 7:30 tonight."

"I'll be there, Al," she said with a warm smile.

He glanced around the room, looking for the painting, but couldn't find it. He didn't want to confront her directly until he'd worked out what this whole Alexis handwriting thing was. It would have to wait until that evening.

When he left, he called the rest of the Group, Ron McGuire, Alexis Berry-McGuire, Paul Spears, and, of course, Jonty and Philippa, and invited them to join him for dinner at Bianchi's that evening.

He explained to Philippa what he had done and why, and she was more than happy to go along with it. She was a little concerned about Jonty going, but Al heard him in the background telling her it was nonsense, he could use a good dinner.

The rest of the afternoon passed in a blur.

Al went over his theory in his head numerous times.

He ran it by Jake, who agreed it made total sense.

He called Cassie, to let her know he'd be driving home that evening rather than taking the train. He didn't want to hang around after wrapping up the case. Who knew who was affiliated with whom?

If Alexis had managed to leave the drug-laced coffee for Jonty in the house, without anyone noticing, she could have done it in the night. He certainly didn't remember seeing it the night of the wake. Obviously, the security systems were not as hot as he'd thought. Or… well, that would have to wait for later.

He called the local police to let them know he had new information for them about Milton Arrowsmith's murder. He insisted on being put through to the lead detective on the case, but was told he was out, and wouldn't be in until the morning.

"Seriously, it's real important," Al said.

"I'm sure it is," the cop at the other end of the line said, in a tone like Al was some nut case he had to humor. Al could hear the sound of him eating, and wondered if it was the stereotypical cop's donut. "I'll tell him just as soon as he gets in."

"Fine."

Once he was sure he had his theory all straight, Al went upstairs to get changed. He pulled on his favorite shirt only to find it was horribly creased. Thankfully Beth helped him out by ironing it.

Twenty minutes later, after he was showered and shaved, he stood in the bedroom, straightening his tie in the closet mirror.

Louis sat by the bed.

"I'm gonna miss you, pal," Al said. "Though it seems Penelope and ya' are gettin' on just fine. Is Philippa gonna' send me emails about little puppies in the future, huh?"

He chuckled, and ruffled Louis under his chin. "Wish I could take ya' home, sonny, but Red would have a fit." Red, Al and Cassie's Doberman pinscher, was a wonderful dog, but rather possessive about Al and loved to be the center of attention. Al was certain bringing Louis home with him would not go down well with Red.

Then he packed his suitcase. He heard Jonty and Philippa arrive a little later, as planned, and get showered and ready for the evening meal. He was going in his own rental car, so he decided to take off a little early. He wanted to be the first one to arrive.

Thankfully the parking outside Bianchi wasn't too bad, despite it being in the center of the city, and he managed to find a parking spot within a few minutes. The restaurant was right up his alley in terms of ambience and décor.

Although he did like the '*Italian nonna*' style restaurants when he was craving a bit of comfort food, he also thought they were often a little cliché. Bianchi's was nothing of the sort. It was all metal and glass with potted plants, and it had a wonderful fountain wall that changed colors under flashing LED lights.

But that didn't mean it wasn't authentic. All of the staff were Italians, and when he was handed a menu, he was very pleased with the selection of food offered. Sitting by himself at the large table he'd reserved, he allowed himself one small glass of red wine.

The one thing that wasn't authentic was the bowl of extra virgin olive oil, balsamic vinegar, and the warm bread to go with it. That seemed to only be served outside Italy. But Al didn't care if it wasn't the real deal. He totally understood why it was popular, and enjoyed his starter with gusto.

He'd already picked out his main course within moments of sitting down – Malloreddus with a rosemary ragu sauce and Campidanese sausage. It had been at long time since he'd had malloreddus, a gnocchi creation made from semolina flour. They were a Sardinian favorite, and his great uncle, who was from the island, had made them on occasion.

There were plenty of other tempting options, and he always liked to try the pizza in every Italian restaurant he went to, seeking out the best of the best, so he changed his mind more than once.

But he didn't have much time to deliberate over the main course options.

Before long, the members of the Group were arriving in their finery, with no idea of what was about to happen.

First to come were Ron and Alexis. He made small talk with them about pretty much nothing. It was one of his gifts from his previous life in the Mafia. Sometimes you had to hang around and talk to shady characters, and the best thing to do was talk about innocuous subjects. They spoke about Louis, and pets in general.

Then came Cilly and her boyfriend Gabriel Barroso, followed shortly after by Paul Spears, then, finally, Jonty and Philippa.

They all ordered wine, and toasted Milton.

"May he rest in peace," Jonty said.

Al cleared his throat. "As ya' know, we're here 'cause I'm leavin', but we're also here for another reason." They all looked at him expectantly. "'Cause the paintin' thief, Milton's murderer, and the person who drugged Jonty are all in this room."

Everyone gasped, even those who he knew were guilty.

"You mean they're different people?" Philippa said, frowning.

"Yep," Al said. "I was as surprised as ya' are." He paused, looking at each of them in turn, hoping against hope he was right.

"Well, go on!" Philippa said breathlessly.

CHAPTER NINETEEN

Al turned to Cilly. "Yer' the paintin' thief."

"No, I'm not!" Cilly protested. "Why would I steal a painting that was meant to be auctioned for charity? No, you're confused. Where's your proof?"

"How dare you accuse my girlfriend!" Gabriel Barroso said, standing up and pointing his finger at Al.

"I got the surveillance footage from the hotel," Al said, "showin' ya' leavin' the penthouse with the paintin'."

"Yes, I did leave with a painting, because Milton told me to take it back to the art dealer!" she said. "If you looked closely, you'll see I brought three paintings into the house, which I'd brought from a friend who left them at the art dealer for me to pick up. Milton took a look at them all, and didn't like one, so he sent it back."

"So why didn't ya' take it back to the art dealer?" Al said.

"I did," she said, but she blushed terribly. She wasn't a very good liar. Everyone stared at her, and she burst into tears. "All right, all right, I did take it. I took the painting and kept it, but I didn't kill

Milton, I swear it!"

"It's okay, it's okay," Gabriel said, pulling her into a hug and stroking her hair.

"And ya' lied to me," Al said. "You came over the day of the wake and concocted a story 'bout Philippa and Jonty killin' Milton that was completely untrue. That was just to throw the scent off ya', right, Cilly?"

"Cilly!" Philippa said. "How could you do such a thing?"

"Debt is a terrible thing," Al said. When Cilly and Gabriel looked up at him in shock, he said, "Ya' shouldn't leave paperwork lyin' 'round when visitors come over."

"You were going to sell it?" Alexis said, aghast. "Profiting off of your own friend's death? That's despicable!"

"Ya' ain't much better, Alexis, are ya'?" Al said. "Puttin' a date rape drug in Jonty's coffee so that ya' could go ahead and scoop up his paintings."

"What?" Alexis said, paling.

"Darling?" Ron said.

"You!" Jonty said, casting a threatening look at Alexis. "Al, how did you find out?"

"Handwritin' analysis," Al said. "I got her to write a little somethin' for me, and it was a 100% match with the note that was left with the coffee."

Alexis babbled, "No, no, I swear on my life I had nothing to do with this."

"Oh really?" Al said. He pulled the note For Jonty out of his pocket and held it up. "So why was this note left on the top of the box of coffee was used to drug Jonty? It's in yer' handwritin'."

Alexis gasped. "No. No way." She looked at Jonty with murder in her eyes. "You're, you're setting me up."

"I don't know what you're talking about," Jonty said.

"I do," Al said. He really didn't, but he didn't want Jonty to get the upper hand. He did have the most damning evidence on him, though. "Because you, Jonty, were the one who rode up in the elevator with the box of chocolates. You hid 'em in yer' satchel, but jes' a millisecond before Milton answered the door, ya' reached into yer' bag, and began to pull them out.

"Cops musta' missed it. I went over that tape a hundred times to make sure I got it. And even then, I weren't sure. I had to have the security team zoom right in on it, 'cause it was jes' a tiny view, right under yer' finger. But, sure enough, it was purple with gold letterin'."

"Liar," Jonty snarled. "It was Milton's son who killed him. I have proof."

"Ya' ain't got no proof at all," Al said. "I done my diggin' into that, too. This so-called Trent guy is actually named Hunter Stephan. I saw it by accident when he showed me his flight details. He weren't even in Vancouver at the time of the murder, and he was never captured on camera at the hotel. I don't know who he is. Jes' some conman probably here to try his luck fer the money. But he ain't Milton's son, and he didn't kill him."

Jonty leaned back in his chair with a smirk. Philippa was looking at Al, fury in her face. "So…" Jonty said. "This supposed murder of Milton. How would I carry it out? And more to the point, why?"

"To get yer' dirty hands on his money, of course…"

"I'm afraid you're tragically mistaken," Jonty said. "Because I'm not seeing a penny of Milton Arrowsmith's estate. It's all going to his parents under the terms of his trust which provides that his estate goes to his closest living relatives, which in this case, are his parents."

"But ya' didn't know about his parents when Milton was murdered," Al said. "You didn't even know they existed."

"I did," he said. "If you remember, Al, I'm quite the investigator myself. I got in contact with them to get them to come take their money."

Al paused. "I don't believe a word yer' sayin'. Ya' said that night ya' knew about Trent. But there was no Trent. He was Hunter Stephan all along."

Al's thoughts were twisting themselves into knots.

This had been his theory:

Milton had made Jonty the trustee of his estate.

Jonty had then killed him with a poisoned chocolate thinking if Milton had no living relatives, he, as trustee, could highjack the trust fund and no one would know. He'd made the ricin from Philippa's stash of castor beans.

Cilly had stolen the painting because she was in debt, and it had nothing to do with the murder.

At some point along the line, Cilly and Alexis had teamed up to steal more paintings. Maybe Alexis had been involved from the beginning. That's why he saw them whispering in the corner at the wake.

Cilly had come over before the wake with her ridiculous tall-tale to put him off the scent. Alexis had drugged Jonty, so she could go and take his paintings. When he'd returned from the offices of Icon X, he'd made a call and discovered she'd been at the art dealer's gallery that morning.

But then, maybe she freaked out when Al turned up at her office, and she'd given him evidence that it was Cilly, so suspicion would be taken away from her.

Al also had an inkling that maybe Alexis was the one Jonty was having an affair with. That led him to an idea.

"Well, fine, ya' didn't want his inheritance, but you did want the painting," Al said. "You and Alexis, yer' lover, teamed up with Cilly to kill Milton and steal the paintin'."

There was a long pause, and both Alexis and Jonty started laughing.

Al wanted the ground to open up and swallow him.

"A painting worth a quarter of a mil!" Jonty said with a snort. "Do you know how much I'm worth?"

"Oh, no," Alexis said, laughing so much she could barely catch her breath. "This is too much. Nice job hiring this bozo as a PI, Philippa!"

Philippa looked to Jonty. "Is this true? Is this the hussy you've been sleeping with?"

"Don't call my wife a hussy!" Ron McGuire said.

This started a full-blown argument between the three couples.

Al sank down to his chair, humiliated. He was so sure he'd gotten it right. Now, even though he had the surveillance evidence of Jonty, he was beginning to doubt that conclusion as well. Everything seemed so strange and alien. He could have lifted his hand in front of his face, counted his five fingers, and doubted he'd gotten it right.

He glanced across the table, and saw Paul Spears eyeing him, while everyone else argued. They shared a look for a moment, and Al thought Paul Spears felt sorry for him. He burned inside. It was the most awful feeling.

A waiter came over and clapped his hands loudly. "Excuse me!" he said. "We're getting complaints from other tables. Can you all quiet down, please, or else you'll have to leave."

"Don't worry, we're leaving," Gabriel said, putting his arm around Cilly and pulling her up. "And never speaking to any of you again."

"I'm putting in a report about the painting," Jonty said, looking Cilly up and down in disgust. "You dirty thief."

"You!" Gabriel pointed his finger right in Jonty's face. "You just try it. We all know you're a murderer."

"Prove it," Jonty spat at him.

"We're leaving, too," Philippa said. She shot a look at Al. "I brought you into my home to find out what was going on, not to betray us. I hope you've removed everything from our home."

"I have," Al said, feeling like a hollow shell. How could he have gotten it so wrong?

He expected Alexis and Ron to leave right away, too, but Alexis leaned over the table. "Al, you were right about the note. I did write it, but a long time ago. It was with a bottle of wine I gave Jonty for his birthday, from Ron and me. He must have kept it, then drugged himself and pinned it on me."

"Uh-huh," Al said. He couldn't think straight. It was as if someone had landed a huge roundhouse punch right in his face, and he was still reeling. He could barely process what Alexis was saying.

"And I didn't steal any painting," she said. "Trust me, I'm not involved at all."

Al got enough of his wits back about him to ask, "Why were you at the art dealer's this morning, then?"

"To see about a new painting for my office," she said. "I'm being promoted to CEO."

"Oh. Congrats."

"Let's go, darling," Ron said quietly. He patted Al sympathetically on his way out. "I don't think you're wrong about Jonty," he said in a low voice.

Having Ron be kind to him made it all the worse.

In the end, it was just Al and Paul Spears sitting across from each other. The waiter came up to take their order, and asked if they would care to move to a smaller table.

"Sure," Paul Spears said. "Let's."

Al was surprised. "Okay."

They were moved to a table for two further back in the restaurant. Al decided against the malloreddus, and went with his ultimate comfort food, pepperoni pizza. He was in such a bad place he barely noticed what Paul ordered.

After a few moments, Al took a sip of wine, and laughed shakily. "That went well."

"It's not your fault," Paul said quickly. "You only have half the information."

"Tell me 'bout it."

Paul looked uncomfortable and shifted in his seat.

"Ya' know somethin', don'tcha?" Al asked, his investigative instincts kicking in.

Paul looked up at him, shocked.

"Ya' do!" Al said.

"I think you're right about Jonty," Paul said.

"But there ain't no motive," Al said. "And even if there was a trial, one thing I know is that juries need a motive. They don't legally, but they always want one. I've seen so many cases where all the evidence is there, but with no motive, the jury acquits. The paintin' thing I said… it didn't make sense."

"I know the motive," Paul said. "I didn't say anything, because I didn't have the evidence. But now you have it, and paired with the motive I know, it's a done deal."

"What is it?" Al said, leaning forward in his seat.

"Jonty and Milton were having an affair."

Al fell back in his seat, shocked to the core. He was breathless for a few seconds. He hadn't expected that. "What? How do ya' know?"

"When I was friends with Milton, he'd always drop hints about his lover. His lover who bought him a Rolex watch and a set of diamond cufflinks. I asked to be introduced, but he said his lover wanted to keep it a secret, because he was married to a woman. He always told me that the man was going to leave his wife.

"Then we stopped talking, so I didn't think anything more about it. But once, the Group was at Philippa and Jonty's for an event. Philippa had already gone to bed, and everyone was leaving. I let Penelope out to do her business for the night, and saw Jonty and Milton on the balcony. They weren't doing anything, but they were close. Too close. They didn't see me."

"Oh, man." Al processed the information. "Jonty… when he was drunk at the wake… he said somethin' to Trent 'bout marriage bein' a misery, and not bein' able to divorce because of the financial implications. So… so Milton was puttin' pressure on Jonty to leave Philippa, and Jonty killed him for it?"

"I think so," Paul said.

Al shook his head. "We need stronger evidence."

"I know just where you can go for that."

CHAPTER TWENTY

Kiran Chong was very happy to let Al and Paul into Milton's penthouse, especially when Al told him they were very close to having enough evidence to prove who the murderer was.

They went straight into Milton's bedroom, and began to search for the piece of evidence they needed. Paul said there was one place he was certain they'd find something, Milton's diary.

The evidence was in plain sight, right on the nightstand.

"Sure woulda' made my life easier if I'd looked at that the first time I came here with Philippa..." Al said, shaking his head. But he soon realized he wouldn't have been able to interpret the entry.

Paul took the diary from him. "I'm more concerned about the competency of the police. They had this place taped up for days, and they didn't even take his diary?"

"Right!" Al agreed.

"Look, here's the entry for the night before the murder," Paul said, "He wrote, *I've finally told him. I'm not going to be pushed around any longer. He leaves his wife, or I'll tell her. It's as simple as that. I...*"

"Don't read any further," Al said. "That's all we need." His brain kicked into overdrive. "The only other thing we need is evidence he intended to kill Milton with the chocolates. He could say Philippa poisoned 'em, and he didn't know what he was takin' over to Milton."

"True," Paul said. "I hadn't thought of that."

Al sighed. "Time to go back to Philippa's. I wouldn't advise you to come. Jonty might be dangerous."

"That's why I've got to come," Paul said. "I have to be there for Philippa. And to tell her how I feel about her. I wish I'd done it a long time ago."

Al patted him on the back. "Well, I gotta' say, she'd be much better off with ya', and I woulda' said that even before I knew Jonty was a murderer."

A few minutes later Al knocked on the door to the Murdoch home, wishing he had his gun on him. While Jonty had never previously posed a danger, that was because he hadn't been caught. He'd be rattled right now, and rattled killers were very dangerous people.

He was glad they'd gone over there, but then he remembered Philippa and Jonty's previous altercation with the knife. Although Philippa had seemed to be on her husband's side in the restaurant, she would probably have questioned him when they'd gotten home. He hoped things hadn't taken a turn for the worse.

Beth answered the door with wide eyes. "What on earth is going on?" she whispered to Al.

"Where are they?" he asked.

"She's sobbing her heart out in the kitchen," Beth said. "He stormed into his office."

"Okay, let's go see her," Al said.

Beth led them into the kitchen, and Philippa was so deep in her crying she didn't even look up when Al called her name.

"Philippa," he said, louder.

She looked up at him, her face a picture of tear-stained devastation.

"I'm really sorry," Al said.

"It's not your fault."

"I gotta' level with you," Al said. "Jonty was having an affair. You were right, but it was with Milton."

Her eyes widened with shock, and she almost fell off the barstool she was sitting on, leaning her elbow on the counter for support. "No…" she whispered. "Really? Are you sure?" She looked between Al and Paul. Paul, nodded, grim-faced.

Al went over to her and spoke gently. "We got all the information we need to get Jonty put away fer this. I know he's your husband, but…"

"He's not," Philippa said. "He's a liar, a murderer, a cheat, and who knows what else? He's a monster. He's not my husband."

That was exactly what Al wanted to hear. "There's jes' one more thing we need. We gotta' be able to link him to the castor beans. I know the police still have yer' apothecary collection, but could ya' let us into his office?"

She grimaced. "He's the only one with a key. He's in there now. I need a drink."

She went through the hallway to the living room and over to the cabinet where the liquor was kept. Al, Paul, and Beth followed.

"Beth, better lock yerself' in the bathroom," Al said. "We're gonna' confront Jonty, and he could be dangerous. Better yet, go home."

"Okay, I'm going," Beth said. She rushed out to the hallway, and they heard the front door open and close.

Philippa took a huge swig of whiskey right out of the bottle, and grimaced. "Crunch time."

They went back into the hallway, and approached Jonty's office.

"Jonty, dear?" Philippa called out.

"What?" came a savage voice from inside.

"Can I come in, please?"

"No!"

"I need to see you, darling. Please, I believe you. I know you would never kill Milton. I need to tell you something. Please."

There was a long silence, and after a few seconds, a key turned in the lock, and they heard the lock click open. Paul and Al stood on either side of the doorway. As soon as the door opened, Al nodded at Paul, and they both lunged at Jonty. They knocked him back and tried to restrain him while he yelled and thrashed.

Jonty managed to punch Paul in the face, and Paul was rocked back for a moment, dazed. But then he launched forward and gave Jonty an enormous right hook with his closed fist. It took Jonty off his feet, and he fell to the floor, unconscious.

The three of them, Al, Philippa, and Paul, looked down at Jonty, all of them breathing hard.

"Whoa," Al said. "That was quite a punch ya' packed, Paul."

"I'll say," Philippa said quietly.

"No time to waste," Al said. "I'm gonna' look through everythin'. Keep yer' eye on Jonty, in case he comes to."

Al ransacked the desk, looking for anything he could find. And soon he found it. "Aha! A bottle of lye. Used in making ricin. We got it. We're done."

"I'm calling the police," Paul said.

They all watched Jonty, half-expecting him to regain consciousness and try to attack, but he didn't. Paul's punch had been enough for the moment.

"Could be out fer another ten minutes or so, I think," Al said. "When he wakes up, he'll be in cuffs."

EPILOGUE

Al had been back in Seattle for a few months, and was enjoying returning to a normal life. He and Jake had a quiet period in their investigation business and were taking advantage of a relatively free and easy summer.

Although DeeDee was busy with an endless round of summer catering jobs, weddings, garden parties, and company's parties for their employees, she carved out enough time on a weekend to take an evening cruise on the Sound with Jake, Al, and Cassie.

They were in Al's sailboat, and were thoroughly enjoying the feeling of being on the water.

"I feel so darn free," Al said. "Like I ain't got a care in the world."

"I know," Cassie said, snuggling into his shoulder. "It's wonderful. We should do this more often."

"Agreed," DeeDee said, coming up beside them with Jake. "I've been working my tail off this summer. I think in the fall I'll need a good vacation, and I'm booking you all in, like it or not."

They laughed.

"Yes, ma'am," Cassie said.

Jake kissed DeeDee on her cheek. "I'm proud of you, babe. And you definitely deserve a long vacation."

Al's phone vibrated in his pocket. "Hey!" he said. "Philippa's sent me an email." He quickly opened it, and a grin spread across his face. There was a picture of Philippa and Paul sitting next to each other on a sofa, looking happy and in love. Penelope was on Philippa's lap. Louis was on Paul's.

Hi there, Al.

Guess why I'm emailing you?

I'm inviting you to our wedding! Yes!

It's not for a year and a half yet, to make sure my divorce with Jonty goes through properly, but we've set the date, and I wanted to let you know.

We just moved to Montreal, and Paul's gotten a new job here.

We bought a beautiful cottage at the edge of the water, but it's a little old fashioned, so I'm applying myself to making it really beautiful.

Thank you so much, Al, for all you did for me.

I didn't know when I hired you how much you being in my life for a very short time would change everything.

Say hello to Cassie, and your dog Red.

Penelope and Louis are very happy.

Oh, by the way, there has been a shocking development concerning Alexis. Ron left her in the middle of the night and never came back. She discovered the next day that he had cleaned out their bank account and investments to the tune of nearly a million dollars. She was totally devastated.

She had him investigated and learned he wasn't Ron McGuire, a retired brain surgeon, but instead was some sort of an internationally known conman, who is apparently rather famous for stealing large sums of money from unsuspecting women. What a tragedy.

His whereabouts are unknown to the authorities. In fact, they don't even know his true identity. She's filed to have her marriage to him annulled. The police have advised her that Trent Hunter was working in concert with Ron. Not surprising, since Trent disappeared immediately after Milton's murder was solved by you.

Maybe someday when you have a little spare time, you can hunt Ron McGuire down and bring him back to justice, just for old times' sake.

Please RSVP for the wedding when you can.

All our thanks to you,

Philippa and Paul

RECIPES

PEANUT BUTTER POUND CAKE WITH HONEY

Ingredients:
1 cup butter, softened
2 cups sugar
½ cup creamy peanut butter
5 large eggs
¼ cup milk
¼ cup cream
1 tsp, vanilla extract
2 ½ cups flour
½ tsp, salt
1 (10 oz.) bag peanut butter morsels

Icing:
1 (8 oz.) package cream cheese, softened
¼ cup honey
8 tbsp. heavy whipping cream
Optional garnish: chopped dry-roasted peanuts, honey

Directions:
　　Preheat oven to 350. Spray a Bundt pan with cooking spray and dust with flour. In large bowl beat butter, sugar and peanut butter with mixer at medium speed until fluffy (3-4 minutes). Add eggs, one at a time, beating well after each addition. Beat in milk, cream, and

vanilla. In a medium-sized bowl, sift together flour and salt.

Gradually add flour mixture to butter mixture, beating until combined. Stir in peanut butter morsels. Spoon batter into prepared Bundt pan.

Bake 1 hour and 10 - 20 minutes until a wooden pick inserted in center comes out clean. During last 20 minutes of baking, if needed, loosely cover pan with foil to prevent excess browning.

Remove from oven & let pan cool 10 minutes on a wire rack. Remove cake from pan and let cool for one hour on a wire rack.

In a medium bowl, beat cream cheese, honey, and cream with a mixer at medium speed until smooth. Drizzle on top of cake. Garnish with peanuts and honey, if desired.

ROSEMARY FOCCACIA BREAD

Ingredients:
½ cup extra-virgin olive oil
2 garlic cloves, finely minced
1 tbsp. chopped fresh thyme or 1 tsp. dried thyme
1 tbsp. chopped fresh rosemary or 1 tsp. dried rosemary
¼ tsp. freshly ground black pepper
1 cup warm water
2 ¼ tsp. active dry yeast (1 packet)
¼ tsp. honey
2 ½ cups all-purpose flour
½ tsp. fine sea salt

Directions:
In a cold medium-sized skillet, combine olive oil, minced garlic, thyme, rosemary, and black pepper. Place the pan over low heat and cook, stirring occasionally, 5 to 10 minutes or until aromatic, but before the garlic browns. Set aside.

In a large bowl, combine warm water, yeast, and honey. Stir a few times then let sit for 5 minutes.

Add 1 cup of the flour and ¼ cup of the infused garlic-olive oil mixture to the bowl with yeast and honey. Stir 3 to 4 times until the flour has moistened. Let sit for another 5 minutes.

Stir in the remaining 1 ½ cups flour and the salt. When the dough comes together, transfer to a floured board and knead 10 to 15 times until smooth.

Transfer the dough to a large oiled bowl, cover with a warm, damp towel and let rise for 1 hour. (It's best to let the dough rise in a warmer area of your kitchen).

After 1 hour, preheat the oven to 450 degrees.

Use two tablespoons of the remaining garlic-olive oil mixture to oil a 9-inch by 13-inch rimmed baking sheet.

Transfer the dough to the baking sheet then press it down into the pan. Use your fingers to dimple the dough then drizzle the top with the remaining 2 tablespoons of the garlic-olive oil mixture. Let the dough rise for 20 minutes until it puffs slightly.

Bake until golden brown, 15 - 20 minutes. Cool baked focaccia bread on a wire rack. Enjoy!

COQUILLES ST. JACQUES

Ingredients:
2 cups potatoes, peeled and cubed
2 tbsp. butter
2 egg yolks
1 tbsp. cream
2 shallots, finely chopped
2 tbsp. butter

2 tbsp. all-purpose flour
½ cup milk
¼ cup white wine
11 oz. medium-sized scallops (size 15-25), drained and patted dry
1 cup Gruyère cheese, grated
2 tsp. sea salt
Salt and pepper to taste.

Directions:

Place potatoes in a pot and cover with water at least two inches above the potatoes. Add salt. Bring the water to a slow rolling boil and cook the potatoes until fork-tender, about 20 minutes. Drain. Use a potato masher and coarsely crush the potatoes with the butter and egg yolks.

Using an electric mixer, puree the potato mixture with the cream. Season with salt and pepper to taste. Set aside.

Preheat oven to 350 degrees. Over medium heat, soften the shallots in the butter. Add the flour and cook for 1 minute, stirring constantly. Add the milk and wine and bring to a boil while whisking. Cook for 1 minute. Remove from heat and season with salt and pepper. Add scallops and ½ cup of the cheese.

Spoon the scallop mixture into four scallop shells or four small gratin dishes. Dab potatoes around the rim of each. Sprinkle with remaining cheese. Bake for 10 minutes. Finish under the broiler until the cheese and potatoes are golden brown.

TIRAMASU

Ingredients:
1 ¼ cups espresso
6 tbsp. Grand Marnier
40 – 45 ladyfingers (You can usually get these from a supermarket, but they're also available online.)
16 oz. mascarpone cheese

¼ cup dark rum
4 large eggs, separated
½ cup granulated sugar, divided
2 cups heavy cream
½ tsp. pure vanilla extract
1/8 tsp. salt
½ cup unsweetened cocoa powder

Directions:

In a shallow bowl whisk the espresso and Grand Marnier together. Quickly dip half the ladyfingers into the mixture and then remove. You don't want them soggy. Put ½ of the ladyfingers in a 9" x 13" dish. In a medium bowl beat the mascarpone cheese and rum together on medium speed until smooth. Set aside.

Use a double boiler or set a heatproof bowl over a small pot of simmering water over medium-low heat. Whisk the egg yolks and ¼ cup sugar together until light and foamy, about 5 minutes. Remove from heat and pour over mascarpone mixture. Beat on medium speed until combined.

In a medium-sized bowl, using a hand mixer, beat the cream and vanilla extract together until medium peaks form, about 3 - 4 minutes. Fold the whipped cream mixture into the mascarpone mixture.

Beat the egg whites and salt together on medium-high speed until foamy, about 1 minute. Increase speed to high and slowly pour in the remaining ¼ cup sugar. Beat until stiff peaks form, about 4 – 5 minutes. Fold into mascarpone cream.

Spread half of the mascarpone cream evenly over bottom layer of ladyfingers. Dip remaining ladyfingers into the remaining espresso mixture and arrange on top of mascarpone layer. Gently press them down until they're compact. Spread remaining mascarpone mixture over the top. Refrigerate uncovered for 2 - 3 hours.

Remove from the refrigerator and sift cocoa powder over the top. Cover with plastic wrap and refrigerate overnight. When ready to serve, slice chilled tiramisu into servings and plate. Enjoy!

WEEPING TIGER (THAI MARINATED BEEF)

Ingredients:

Steak:
1 garlic clove, diced
4 sprigs cilantro
1 ½ tsp. fresh green peppercorns (Available from specialty store or online.)
1 tsp. fish sauce
1 tsp. light soy sauce
1 tsp. sugar
½ lb. sirloin steak

Chili Sauce:
1 tsp. Thai rice
3 tsp. fish sauce
3 tsp. lemon juice
¼ tsp. sweet chili paste
1 tsp. sugar

1 cup rice, cooked per package instructions

Directions:

Pound together the garlic and cilantro in a mortar and pestle. (If you don't have one, use something heavy to mash them together.) Transfer to a large mixing bowl and combine with the peppercorns, fish sauce, soy sauce, and sugar. Add the steak to the bowl and rub with the marinade. Cool in refrigerator for 20 minutes.

For the chili sauce, toast the rice in a dry wok or pan over low heat until golden brown. Grind to a fine powder using a mortar and pestle. Transfer the toasted rice powder to a small bowl, add the fish sauce, lemon juice, chili paste and sugar, stirring until the sugar has dissolved. Set aside.

Preheat a BBQ grill until hot. Grill the steak for 4 minutes on each side for rare. Let steak stand for 2 minutes and slice into strips. Place sliced strips on a bed of cooked rice, pour sauce over the steak strips. Serve and enjoy!

LEAVE A REVIEW

I'd really appreciate it you could take a few seconds and leave a review of Murder in Vancouver.

Just go to the link below. Thank you so much, it means a lot to me ~ Dianne

http://getbook.at/VANC

Paperbacks & Ebooks for FREE

Go to www.dianneharman.com/freepaperback.html and get your FREE copies of Dianne's books and favorite recipes immediately by signing up for her newsletter.

Once you've signed up for her newsletter you're eligible to win three paperbacks. One lucky winner is picked every week. Hurry before the offer ends!

ABOUT THE AUTHOR

Dianne lives in Huntington Beach, California, with her husband, Tom, a former California State Senator, and her boxer dog, Kelly. Her passions are cooking, reading, and dogs, so whenever she has a little free time, you can either find her in the kitchen, playing with Kelly in the back yard, or curled up with the latest book she's reading. Her award winning books include:

Cedar Bay Cozy Mystery Series

Cedar Bay Cozy Mystery Series - Boxed Set

Liz Lucas Cozy Mystery Series

Liz Lucas Cozy Mystery Series - Boxed Set

High Desert Cozy Mystery Series

High Desert Cozy Mystery Series - Boxed Set

Northwest Cozy Mystery Series

Northwest Cozy Mystery Series - Boxed Set

Midwest Cozy Mystery Series

Midwest Cozy Mystery Series - Boxed Set

Cottonwood Springs Cozy Mysteries

Cottonwood Springs Cozy Mysteries - Boxed Set

Midlife Journey Series

Midlife Journey Series - Boxed Set

The Holly Lewis Mystery Series

Holly Lewis Mystery Series - Boxed Set

Miranda Riley Paranormal Cozy Mystery Series

A Cozy Cookbook Series

Coyote Series

Red Zero Series

Black Dot Series

Newsletter

If you would like to be notified of her latest releases please go to www.dianneharman.com and sign up for her newsletter.

Website: www.dianneharman.com,
Blog: www.dianneharman.com/blog
Email: dianne@dianneharman.com

DIANNE HARMAN

PUBLISHING 4/11/20

DEADLY ACCUSATIONS

BOOK 3

MIRANDA RILEY COZY MYSTERY SERIES

http://getbook.at/DEADLY

A man and a woman found drained of their blood
Local vampires?
Paranormal community says no
A third draining victim is discovered
Agency threatens to fire Miranda
If she doesn't find the killer and make an arrest
She's willing to become bait for the suspected vampire murderer
Will it work?

When the Paranormal Investigative Agency gives Miranda an ultimatum – find the paranormal murderer or be fired – she has to use everything she's been taught to try and catch the culprit.

But are silver bullets, knives, and garlic enough to stop a vampire from another draining?

Add to it her romance with the local Alpha werewolf and her attraction to the Chief of Police. Plus her mother, Eve, is searching for the paranormal who killed Miranda's father many years ago.

Things are definitely getting complicated. Good thing she has her little Corgi, Hank, to help her.

Open your smartphone, point and shoot at the QR code below. You will be taken to Amazon where you can pre-order 'Deadly Accusations'.

(Download the QR code app onto your smartphone from the iTunes or Google Play store in order to read the QR code below.)

Made in the USA
Monee, IL
23 May 2020